W. G. van Tassel Sutphen

The Golficide

And Other Tales of the Fair Green

W. G. van Tassel Sutphen

The Golficide
And Other Tales of the Fair Green

ISBN/EAN: 9783743444003

Manufactured in Europe, USA, Canada, Australia, Japa

Cover: Foto ©Andreas Hilbeck / pixelio.de

Manufactured and distributed by brebook publishing software (www.brebook.com)

W. G. van Tassel Sutphen

The Golficide

[Page 223

"'THE NAME OF THAT BUNKER IS *GRIMSHAW'S GRAVE*'"

The Golficide

and Other Tales of
the Fair Green. By
W. G. VAN T. SUTPHEN
WITH ILLUSTRATIONS

NEW YORK AND LONDON
HARPER & BROTHERS
1898

TO

E. B. S.

CONTENTS

ILLUSTRATIONS

THE GOLFICIDE

THE GOLFICIDE

Morgan Gordon handed his putter to the caddie and walked slowly over to the club-house. This, then, was the ending of his golfing life; this the inglorious issue of the hard-fought conflict. Yet, now that the strain was over, he would not have had it otherwise. The struggle, thank Heaven! was at an end; the fierce, fitful fever had at last burned itself out; to-night he would sleep well. Quickly his mind ran back over the past two years—from the first topped ball down to the short putt that he had only just missed. And oh, how short a putt it was!—a shade under six inches!—and that fool, Robinson Brown, had made a

3

snap-shot of it, confound his impudence !
Well, it was all over now, and he drew a
long breath of relief, subtly tempered
by the impalpable sadness of an infinite regret. Unconsciously, and in all
but the accomplished fact, Morgan Gordon was already the golficide, bunkered
at the last hole and by his own hand.

It was as a member of the Marion
County Club that Morgan Gordon had
begun his brief career of misdirected
golf. And yet the man had been sincere
in his humble way. He had not made
golf a stalking-horse for his social ambitions, nor yet a clothes-horse upon which
to hang red coats and incongruous tar-
tans. Golf had really been to him an
ideal, pure, fresh, and all-absorbing. He
had embraced it with ardor, he had pursued it with unwearying zeal, and, until
this fatal day, he had never absolutely
despaired of its final attainment. But
now—

And yet, after all, his story was but
the common one—his disappointments

4

and trials had differed only in degree
from those usually attendant upon a
golfer's education. He had lost balls
and broken clubs and fallen among
bunkers just as everybody else did ; but
then, in the beginning, we were all duffers together, and reflection upon that
undeniable fact was calculated to take
the sting out of much foozling.

But as time went on a certain process
of differentiation worked out its inevitable results. Certain players began to
hit the ball clean and to make the round
in double figures, and presently one of
them became the acknowledged champion of the club. Morgan Gordon only
smiled at this ; he felt that he was perfecting his style and could afford to
wait.

The weeks slipped away, the gap continued to grow wider and wider, and one
day the Green Committee announced
that henceforth the playing members
would be divided into classes A, B, and
C. At the foot of class C stood the

name of Morgan Gordon, and, beholding it, he smiled no longer. It was time to buckle down to real work.

Now, it is a pretty firmly established fact that to succeed at golf one must give his undivided attention to the task. There can be no half-hearted allegiance to "Our Lady of the Links." The goddess of golf is a terribly exacting mistress, and she accepts no devotion unless it be absolute and unqualified. Least of all can she brook the presence of a rival. It was none of Morgan Gordon's business that Alice Townley took no interest in golf. Of course she was a member of the club, and occasionally she condescended to a mixed foursome, but she did not really enjoy or play the game. To her peculiarly constituted nature golf did not appeal—a sorrowful fact, and yet, withal, an incontrovertible one. *De golfibus non est disputandum.*

Now, I repeat that all this was none of Morgan Gordon's business, and it would have been the better for his iron play if he had not attempted to meddle with it. But we all make mistakes, and out of purest loyalty to the *cause* Morgan Gordon set himself to convert the obstinate Miss Townley. Her attitude towards the game was inexplicable. He resented it ; he told himself that he did not believe in it, even as a casual variation upon the eternal feminine. The rebel *must* be brought to submission.

He tried friendly argument (still out of pure zeal, mind you), and he failed. He engaged two professionals to play a purely spectacular match for her especial edification, and she did not even come to see it. He offered to teach her his own swing, and she only smiled. It was too bad, but he could not deceive himself. His unwearying patience, his unwavering enthusiasm had accomplished absolutely nothing. Between him and Alice Townley there was a great golf fixed.

Strange, is it not, that this untoward circumstance should have touched Mor-

gan Gordon so nearly? And, stranger
yet, he had received no assistance whatever in his missionary work from the
one whose interests he was so loyally
striving to further. Alas, poor fellow!
he had overlooked the fact that the goddess of golf and the immovable Miss
Townley were both of the inscrutable
feminine persuasion, and that he was
really the last person in the world who
could hope to mediate between them.
It was stupid, too, of the goddess; she
should never have allowed him to make
the attempt. Still, in that case there
would have been no story to tell.

Mr. Morgan Gordon was a person of
some decision of character, and he was
not yet ready to give up the fight. The
autumn handicap was about six weeks
off, and the prize was an exceedingly
handsome piece of plate. If he could
go to Alice Townley with that cup in
his hand, there is no telling what surprising results might be effected. No
woman in her senses could fail to see

its possibilities as a claret-jug in a limited menage, and its lustrous magnificence would unquestionably adorn even the humblest of cottage side-boards.

In the pursuance of this ingenious policy, Morgan Gordon immediately gave up the lease of his office in the city, made arrangements to take all his meals at the club-house, and placed himself under the care of the resident professionals. All for golf, you will please remember. My hero's sincerity of purpose must not be questioned for a moment, and it was certainly never doubted by himself.

Six weeks of unremitting toil with brassey and niblick, and the handicap was on. There was only one thing that could possibly prevent Morgan Gordon's triumph, and of course that one thing happened. "Our Lady of the Links" had a fit of the sulks, and Morgan Gordon couldn't hit a ball. There had been twenty-six entries (six of them from the gentler sex), and, lo! Morgan Gordon's

score led all the rest. Disgraceful! and
how Alice Townley's eyes had flashed
scornful fire as the totals went up,
chalked with uncompromising plainness
upon the big club blackboard! No wonder that Morgan Gordon's heart was very
bitter as he made that short journey
over to the club-house.

He picked out a seat in the darkest
corner of the smoking-room and puffed
savagely at a big black cigar, while he
reflected upon his late discomfiture.
Certainly "Our Lady of the Links"
had not been kind; she must have
taken his well-intentioned efforts to
convert Miss Townley as a deliberate
slight to her own charms, and, womanlike, had sought to punish him. But
this time the goddess had gone a trifle
too far, by S. Andrews! She had, indeed, and he would not stand it! Too
long already had he suffered from the
unreasonable caprices of this *belle dame
sans merci*, who held out glittering al-
lurements in the guise of triple-plated

electro, and then delivered up her cred-
ulous worshippers to the torments of un-
frequented side-hazards and unfathomable bunkers. Morgan Gordon's heart
was very sore as he thought of these
things, and he began to wonder if, after
all, the game had been worth the candle
(with which he had been wont to practise putting after dark). Might there
not be better things in life than a two-
hundred-yard drive? nobler ambitions
than holing in three off the iron?

He rose and walked to the window.
Alice Townley was sitting in a secluded
corner of the piazza, and half unconsciously Gordon found himself staring
hard at the gracious picture that she
made against the green-and-scarlet background of the trumpet-vines. What a
pretty girl she was, to be sure! What
on earth had he been looking at all
these months? What, indeed, but a
filthy piece of battered gutta-percha,
which, after all, he very seldom hit.
Gracious heavens! Why should he have

been wasting his time "addressing" a miserable ball when he might have been talking to a woman like Alice Townley? Why should his left foot know or care what his right foot was doing, so long as his "stance" was at her side? By Jove! and there was that idiot Robinson Brown making up to her now.

He hardly knew how it had all come about so quickly, but there he was in that secluded corner, and he had just finished asking Alice Townley to be his wife. She was speaking slowly and distinctly, but for the moment the words sounded unintelligibly in his ears. What was she saying? In those calmly modulated sentences there was not a trace of the conventional surprise, of the maidenly confusion which might very properly have been expected under the circumstances. No one knew better than Morgan Gordon himself that he was by long odds the most eligible bachelor in all Lauriston, and his declaration had certainly been precipitate and calculated to confuse even so well-balanced a young woman as Alice Townley. But she was speaking, and he must force himself to listen.

"You cannot deny that you are still a golfer," repeated this extraordinary young person. "Influenced by a momentary irritation, you have persuaded yourself into thinking that I am of more importance to your future happiness than even the perfecting of your iron play. I give you all credit for honesty; you think that you are sincere in what you say, and yet I cannot, dare not trust you. Go back to your golf and forget me; believe me, it will be better thus for us both."

Morgan Gordon looked at her in amazement. "I had about decided to give up golf for good," he said, quickly.

"Give it up! You resigned twice from the club last year, did you not?"

"Yes."

"Three times, to my personal knowledge, you sacrificed your entire collection of clubs to the fury of the moment, and once you went so far as to give me your red coat to be made up into pincushions for a charity bazar. And yet you are still playing."

Morgan Gordon looked very sober. "Well, and what of that?"

"Can you ask me such a question, Morgan Gordon? Do you not realize that you are a slave, bound hand and foot in the most hopeless of thraldoms? And yet you ask me to be your wife, you who have foozled away the best years of your life, entangled in long grass, buried in cuppy lies, bunkered for days together in the unspeakable depths of the *Pons Asinorum*. Never! Morgan Gordon. I may live and die Alice Townley, but never, never will I be any man's golf widow!"

Morgan Gordon was silent. He could not but recognize the truth in those stinging words. She was right, a thousand times right. In the vivid lightning

14

that flashed from her stormy eyes he had
caught a glimpse of himself and of his
real position. He was, indeed, a golfiac
and the slave of his own niblick. He
bowed his head in speechless bitterness.

"Perhaps you might join a tennis
club; it is just a chance, but it might
be worth while. It cured Jim Ryder."

"I did try it for a month," said Gordon, timidly. "You remember that I
was expelled because I appeared at the
courts, on three successive days, disguised in knickerbockers."

"I remember," said Miss Townley,
softly.

The sudden tenderness in her voice
emboldened him. "Don't you think
that if you should take me in hand—"
he stopped abruptly, for her face had
grown hard again.

"And commit the most supreme act of
folly of which even a woman is capable!"
She laughed scornfully, and Gordon
looked abashed. She went on quickly:
"There! I did not mean to hurt you;

but, believe me, the thing is impossible.
Heavens! have I not seen it all a thousand times before? There are the Robinson Browns. Could any woman have
done more for the man she loved? I
called at the house yesterday and was
received in the butler's pantry, because,
forsooth, the drawing - room had been
turned into a putting-green for rainy-
day practice. Alderson! When Kitty
Crake married him, did she ever suspect
that the day would come when there
would be a cleek in every room and a
captive ball in the art - gallery? You
depend upon my love and prayers to
deliver you when there is not a patent
iron ever forged which could put you
on the 'Island' green under double figures? No, Morgan, it cannot be. I do
not deny that I might have cared for
you—that I do care for you now, if you
will have it so—but I say again that I
dare not trust you. Pledges! Oaths!
What are mere words upon which to
build our hopes for future happiness?

A trial-drive here, a practice-putt there, and the next handicap would see you again at the bottom of the list. No; it cannot, cannot be !"

"Then there is no hope for me ?"

"I have heard men talk of golficide," returned Miss Townley. "It sounds as though there might be something in it."

"Something not very nice," said Gordon, paling slightly. "It makes me feel a bit queer even to think of it."

Miss Townley looked at him steadily. "I thought as much," she said, icily.

Gordon flushed up at that. "You think that I don't really want to be cured, but you are mistaken. I was only wondering if the agonies of a golfer's dissolution were in any degree commensurate with the torments of his birth and early years. As a golficide I might be worse off than I am now."

Miss Townley looked annoyed. "Very possibly," she said, briefly.

"It's a big risk."

"A tremendous one, no doubt. I

shouldn't dream of asking you to take it."

"But I have already done so," answered Morgan Gordon, his face aglow with a new and high resolve. "Be the issue what it may, I commit golficide this very night, and remember that I shall look to you for my reward," he added, meaningly.

Miss Townley blushed, but she met his steadfast gaze frankly. "I shall be at home any time after ten to-morrow," she said, in a half whisper, for the piazza was now filling up rapidly and the tea-trays were appearing on every side.

Morgan Gordon withdrew into the background, his breast dilating with strange emotions. He had actually asked a girl to be his wife, and he had definitely determined upon golficide. Curiously enough, it was the taking of this second step that moved him the more deeply. To play golf no more! Why, it was like the beginning of a new life. Incredible as it may seem, he no

longer felt any desire to play; no, not
even if he could be a medal man and go
around in 78 or under. Morgan Gordon
gasped; he realized that he was a free
man again, and he could have shouted
aloud in the pure ecstasy born of a great
deliverance. He reflected, however, that
there were a good many people in smart
clothes standing about, and they would
not understand; they might even look
surprised. So he contented himself with
ordering up his T-cart and throwing an
unutterable look in Miss Townley's direction as he drove off; also, a five-dollar
bill to the groom, which was not too
much, considering that the man had a
large family.

After dinner Morgan Gordon went up
to his room, leaving instructions that he
was not to be disturbed. He pulled a
chair in front of the fire and set himself
to consider the situation. Somehow he
felt a vague disquietude in his newly
taken position, and the first fervor of
enthusiasm had sensibly cooled. It was

all very well for Alice Townley to talk golficide, but it was a pity that she could not see that the game had its good points. She was asking a tremendous lot of him ; and just then a demon came and whispered softly in his ear that a loose grip with the right hand was a certain panacea for all sorts of bad driving. It was a tempting, a plausible suggestion, and Morgan Gordon wondered that he had not thought of that before. And it was so simple, such an easy thing to try.

With a great effort of will he put the temptation behind him. He had passed his word and the thing must be done. Must be done ! And how on earth was he to do it? He suddenly realized that he had not the remotest conception of what golficide really was ; he had pledged himself to solve a problem whose very terms were unknown to him. Could anything be more ridiculous?

For a long time Morgan Gordon sat and pondered upon this knotty point.

What was this golficide to which he had committed himself? Resigning from the club, breaking his pet driver, giving away his stock of balls; he had tried all these ordinary methods, as Alice Townley had but just now reminded him. Golficide was not to be accomplished by these puerile expedients; it must be something far more radical and enduring in its results.

He might resort to the heroic measure of amputating a limb, but he remembered having heard of various armless and legless prodigies in the world of golf who were devoted to the sport, and who managed to play a very fair game in spite of their anatomical deficiencies. To overgolf himself, was a second thought, and for the moment an attractive one. But such a remedy could not afford immediate relief, and would not satisfy the exacting Miss Townley. Finally, he might fall upon the point of his niblick, after the fashion of King Saul at Gilboa, but such an

act involved physical self-destruction;
and he remembered with a little thrill
that some one besides himself had now
an interest in his life. It was all a muddle, and the more he smoked and pondered, the more of a muddle it became.
And so, puzzled and dispirited, Morgan
Gordon ordered up a late supper of
golden buck and a bottle of stout, and
having disposed of these simple refresh-
ments, he decided to go to bed and trust
to chance and dreams for an inspiration.

It was a strange half-waking, half-
sleeping state into which Morgan Gordon presently fell. He remained conscious of his own personality and of the
familiar surroundings of his room, and
yet, little by little, some kind of a change
was certainly taking place. At first he
felt only a vague surprise as the walls
of the chamber began to widen and to
recede into the night, but now he could
plainly see the stars shining above his
head, and his comfortable spring mat-
tress had suddenly developed extraor-

dinary qualities of knobbiness and an-
gularity. Absurd! but that really felt
like a stone under the small of his back,
and he tried to turn over. Ugh! there
was a lot of sand up his sleeve, and a
bunch of stinging nettles had taken the
place of his pillow. With an exclama-
tion of impatience Morgan Gordon
opened his eyes, and it was just as he
had expected; this was not his bed at all,
but that unspeakable and loathly sand-
bunker of the Marion County course,
which men call *Pons Asinorum*. Heavens! he should know it well enough by
this time; there was not a day of his
golfing life that he had not visited it
at least once, and his trusty niblick
was well acquainted with every square
inch of its accursed surface. But this
was the middle of the night, and he had
certainly not been golfing. What did it
mean?

With increasing impatience he tried
to rise, and then perceived that he was
buried up to his waist in the loose sand.

More than that, it was rapidly drifting higher and higher, and threatening to overwhelm him completely. Horrors! and he had not a tool or a digging instrument of any kind. In despair he threw out his arms and shouted wildly for assistance. No one appeared in answer to the call, but his hand encountered something cold and hard. He recognized it at once; it was his own niblick. Strange! but never mind, he knew how to use that particular club, and he at once set vigorously at work to extricate himself. The sand flew in showers. There! he could move his right leg a little; another desperate effort and he had wriggled it free.

Five minutes later Morgan Gordon crawled painfully out of the *Pons Asinorum* bunker, drew a long breath of relief, and gazed eagerly about him. It was indeed the golf course of the Marion County Club; it was unquestionably the middle of an unusually dark night, and yet the links were crowded with shadowy, moving figures, great divots of turf hurtled unceasingly through the murky air, and the crack of drivers and the ring of irons resounded from every side. Morgan Gordon glanced over at the first tee. Surely he knew the player who was preparing to strike off ; yes, it was certainly Bingley, an ex-member of the club. Gordon walked up and addressed him by name.

"You !" exclaimed Mr. Bingley, looking at Gordon with a surprise certainly unaffected. "You here !"

"An explanation on your part would be more in order," retorted Gordon. "You're not a member of the club and haven't been for two years."

Mr. Bingley smiled in an aggravating way. "Where do you think you are ?" he demanded, coolly.

"Why, at the Marion County Golf Club," began Morgan Gordon, and then stopped, irresolute and puzzled. It was the familiar scene of the County Club grounds, and then again it was not.

Things looked distorted in the dim light, definite landmarks had arbitrarily resolved themselves into unknown shapes, hills had sunk into formless hollows, and valleys had been exalted into Alpine heights. "But it *is* the County Club," repeated Morgan Gordon, weakly. He felt disquieted, even afraid.

"Just as you like, but at this particular time of night the privileges of the course belong exclusively to the Honorable Company of Passed and Qualified Golficides. You ought to know that well enough."

"The Honorable Company of Passed and Qualified Golficides!" The words fell with startling significance upon Morgan Gordon's ears. With what strange company had he now foregathered? He stared hard at Bingley and then hastily drew back. The figures painted upon the sand-box could be plainly read right through that gentleman's ample person.

"Then there is such a thing?" faltered Morgan Gordon.

"Such a what?"

"Golficide." This last in an awed whisper.

"Why, of course," returned Bingley, complacently. "Every mother's son of 'em there is a golficide, and a good one, too." He indicated, with a comprehensive wave of the hand, the dim figures that moved among the shadows. "I'm one myself—qualified last August."

"But—but aren't they playing—playing golf, I mean?"

"That depends upon what you call golf, my dear fellow. They are certainly playing at it, and, in fact, we meet here every night for regular practice, with hours from midnight to cock-crow. And Sunday play, too," he added, with a sigh. "We fought and protested against it as long as we could, but the *Colonel* insisted."

"The *Colonel*?"

"Yes ; *Bogey*, you know, and a regu-

lar slave-driver he is, too. How I hate
the smooth, oily devil, with his eternal
three off the iron, and no allowance for
a bad lie." Mr. Bingley scowled savagely, and tried to kick an inoffensive wa-
tering-pot into a cocked hat. But his
shadowy foot passed harmlessly through
the material tin ; there was not even a
scratch upon its painted sides.

"It's a little different from what I
had expected," said Morgan Gordon,
hesitatingly. "I had always supposed
that a man committing golficide had
made an end of it—of his golf, I mean."

"And a very common error among
you materialists," retorted Bingley. "It
all depends upon *how* you have golfed,
and there is an immortality for the
medal man as well as for the duffer.
Col. Bogey himself was a scratch man
at St. Andrews for years and years."

"St. Andrews? I thought that was
where the good golfers went when they
died."

"So they do. The bad ones, and we

who have had the temerity to take matters into our own hands, come here."

"Rather a reflection upon the Marion County course," said Gordon, indignantly, "and I don't think that the Green Committee would be pleased if they knew of it."

"On the contrary, the selection is in the nature of a compliment," smiled Bingley. "This is only the intermediate state, don't you know, and we must have a place where we can be sure of getting our afternoon tea regularly. The actual golfing inferno, the final destination of the incorrigible, is of course the club at ——," and Bingley whispered into Gordon's shrinking ear a name that stands high upon the roster of the U. S. G. A.

Morgan Gordon trembled like a leaf. "I have played that course myself," he said, faintly.

"We all have," said Bingley, with a sardonic smile, "and yet there are people who still doubt if there be an actual place of eternal torment.

An electric bell tinkled sharply, and Bingley started. "That's for me," he said, nervously, "and I must be off upon my round. Come along, if you like, and you can examine the workings of our system."

"If you are sure that I sha'n't get in the way," assented Gordon, shyly.

"Not at all," said Bingley, with a grimace. "Getting in the way is my particular number upon the general programme, as you'll soon see for yourself. Come on."

Mr. Bingley kicked his ball off the tee, threw his clubs at a caddie's head, and, accompanied by Morgan Gordon, walked slowly in the direction of the first putting-green. The night, as has been said, was dark, and yet the course was distinctly visible, bathed as it was in a peculiar saffron - colored light. Strangely enough, this unearthly radiance seemed to hang with special persistence over the various sand-bunkers and the other hazards of the fair green, and it possessed a strong and unmistakable odor. Morgan Gordon recognized it at once; yes, it was undoubtedly sulphurous in its origin.

"We have to depend upon the language used by the members to illuminate the grounds," explained Bingley. "And there isn't a better lighted golf course in the country," he added, with a touch of pardonable pride.

"Fore!" The warning rang out sharply from behind, and Morgan Gordon involuntarily ducked, as the ball whizzed close past his head. Bingley fell to the ground, with a yell of pain; the "gutty" had struck him squarely upon the calf of the leg.

"It's outrageous!" exclaimed Gordon, as he assisted the unfortunate Bingley to his feet. "The idea of driving a ball straight at a man! It's a wonder that it didn't hit me."

Bingley looked at Gordon with a

queer expression on his face. "That's the sort of thing I used to do myself—I mean during my golfing life," he said, quietly. "Now everybody on the links is entitled to take a crack at me whenever they please. I don't complain ; it's only justice."

Morgan Gordon began to understand. This was poetic retribution, indeed, but, ah ! how strange and terrible. Poor Bingley !

They had walked a long distance by this time, but the first green still lay far beyond them.

"How long is the course ?" inquired Morgan Gordon.

"It extends to infinity."

"It must take a long time to play around ?"

"An eternity."

"I should think that a man would be liable to overgolf himself," ventured Gordon. But Bingley did not answer. A long brassey shot had just knocked out his last remaining tooth, and he was groaning piteously into his pocket-hand-kerchief.

A man passed them, running with in-credible swiftness through the sulphur-ous gloom. Morgan Gordon gasped with horror as he saw that the poor wretch was wearing a pair of iron shoes that glowed a dull cherry red. The miserable creature came up with his ball, struck at it wildly, and continued upon his head-long course until he was lost to sight in the shadows.

"That was Topley. I think you used to know him," remarked Bingley, in a hard, cold voice.

And, indeed, Morgan Gordon had known the said Topley very well. He had played behind him only too often. That wretched beggar, Topley! he who thought nothing of delaying a whole field of play-ers while he remorselessly fiddled with his grip and tried over his missed putts. He had richly deserved his fate, and, aw-ful as it was, Morgan Gordon could not find it in his heart to pity him.

They were at the green now, and stopped to watch a player who was about to hole out. It was only a six-inch putt; a child could not have missed it. But even as the ball rolled from the putter face the hole moved away, stepping to one side as unostentatiously as though it had been some uninterested spectator, and the ball rested again at that fatal six-inch point. The player looked up into heaven while one might count ten very slowly, and then, with infinite precaution, prepared for another trial. And again the hole moved aside, and there was a sound of rattling tin, as though it were chuckling to itself. And the player! Morgan Gordon looked once upon the face of the Misser of Short Putts, and turned away sick at heart. "I have lived in a glass house myself," thought he.

The view towards the next hole was singularly extended and depressing. A flat, gray table-land stretched to the horizon on every side, and upon its desolate expanse an innumerable company of both men and women crawled painfully about on their hands and knees, while they labored ceaselessly to fit formless pieces of crumbling turf into the irregular holes and cups with which the greensward was pitted for miles around. And through the dusky air came the sound of their crying, exceeding bitter and dolorous.

"These are they who neglected to replace their divots," said Bingley, solemnly ; and Morgan Gordon blanched to a ghastly pallor. He knew that there must be at least a square mile of this sort of thing standing against his name, and it made him feel quite faint. Bingley noticed his distress, and good-naturedly offered him a pull from his pocket-flask. Bitter as gall was the draught, but it brought back the color to Gordon's face, and in a few minutes he was able to go on.

"Water of affliction from the hazard in front of the ninth tee," explained

Bingley. "It's the only beverage out-side of tea that is allowed at the Marion County Club."

They were now passing the *Great Sahara* sand-bunker, and Morgan Gordon saw that it was tenanted by a vast body of men armed with niblicks. Upon the back of each was a huge sack of sand, and some miserable weaklings were bent almost double by their heavy load. But still they toiled on and on, and every now and then a niblick would throw up a shower of sand, which invariably fell straight into the sack upon the play-er's back, and so added to his burden. There was no need for any explanation of this lamentable sight — these were they who had touched sand while in a hazard.

"*My* mountain would completely over-whelm me," thought Morgan Gordon, and his knees grew weak ; he clutched at Bingley for support.

"Come on," commanded his compan-ion ; "the night wears apace ;" and, as one in a dream, Morgan Gordon braced himself and followed.

It was but little that he could afterwards recall of that strange and terrible journey; but still he staggered blindly onward, his feet stumbling upon the dark mountains of illimitable hazards, his eyeballs seared by the blistering, yellow light, his throat gripped hard by the choking, poisonous fumes. On and on, while ever there pressed and thronged about him the unnumbered multitude of the lost. There were men in that dreadful company whom he had met at other clubs; men who were still members of his own; men who had moved away from Lauriston, or who had resigned their memberships; men who had been duffers and men who had been medal-winners. But one mark was common to them all—the blood-red brand of the golficide—the awful seal upon which are written the triple figures and the words that no gentleman should ever use.

There were men there who had often

and deliberately sneaked around bunkers during their brief golfing life. Now, when they drove along what seemed to be a fair and hazardless green, behold! unfathomable abysses suddenly opened and Alpine heights arose before their astonished eyes. And so the ball was trapped, while the duffers beat impotently upon the rocks with their favorite play-clubs, or called down childish curses upon the heads of nameless Green committees. There were others who played with a ball that was *all* top, and others again who ceaselessly pursued through the dun air the whirling fragments of torn score - cards, and still others who wore huge spiked gags in their bleeding mouths, and who mumbled inarticulately to themselves as they stood around the putting-greens and watched their fellows holing out. All these and many more, till the brain of Morgan Gordon reeled, and his heart grew weak as water with the horror and the pity of it all.

And now they were approaching the

home hole, but, marvellous to say, it
was no tin-lined cup, but a huge and
lofty office building that occupied the
familiar putting-green. It was brilliantly lighted from top to bottom, and on
every floor there were endless rows of
office desks, and to them were firmly
chained an army of wan-faced account-
ants. Enormous ledgers lay open before them, and ever as they turned the
leaves continually they did cry: "Nine
and eight are seventeen, and twelve
make twenty-nine."

Morgan Gordon turned to Bingley,
but he had just been laid out stiff by a
hard cleek drive, and a couple of green-
keepers were carrying him off the field.
However, a player who had just finished
his round courteously supplied the desired information. "It is there that we
count up our scores," he said, in a voice
of indescribable sadness. Morgan Gordon would have questioned him further,
but already the unfortunate player had
been hustled into an elevator and im-

mediately whirled up to the twenty-
sixth story, where they deal only in
double figures.

"What are you doing out of your
bunker, sir? Get back to your bunker
immediately—immediately, I say!"

Morgan Gordon looked up. A portly
personage, with cruel, fishy eyes and a
hooked nose, stood before him. Instinctively Morgan Gordon knew that
this could be none other than the
dreaded *Col. Bogey.* What could he
say for himself — how explain the in-
voluntary nature of his presence in
this unholy place? Would it be possible to show proof that he was not a
member of the Honorable Company of
Passed and Qualified Golficides, and,
consequently, not amenable to their dis-
cipline? *Col. Bogey* looked particularly
forbidding as he awaited Morgan Gordon's reply.

"A mistake, I think, sir," faltered the
miserable man.

"*Col. Bogey* never makes a mistake,"

returned that gentleman, with a smile of indescribable malignity.

"But I'm not a golficide!" almost shouted Morgan Gordon. "I'm only a visitor, a house guest of Mr. Bingley's."

Col. Bogey's manner underwent a sudden change to polished suavity.

"Not a golficide? My dear sir, you surprise me. But we can easily help you out; we have all the appliances at hand. Allow me—"

But in a very ecstasy of fear Morgan Gordon had wrenched himself free of that cold and grizzly clutch. He breathed hard and fast.

"I have about decided, indeed I am quite sure, sir, that I had better think it over a little longer. An excellent thing, no doubt, this-er-golficide, but I don't want to do anything which I might have cause to regret. Perhaps next spring, or in a month from now— What's that? Never! Ah!—"

Morgan Gordon lay flat upon his back, having been treacherously assailed from

behind by two of *Col. Bogey's* min-
ions.

"Fool! Duffer!" thundered the in-
censed *Colonel* as he strode over his victim's prostrate form. "Did you think to
play with *Bogey?* Ha! ha! Your curi-
osity will cost you dear enough before
we part company. You have seen al-
together too much, and were you to es-
cape me now there would never be
another golficide from Shinnecock to
Baltusvol. Perish, then, Morgan Gordon, in all the plenitude of your golfing
sins, and they are many, indeed. You
used to sneak around the *Pons Asinorum*, I believe; from henceforth let
each succeeding night find you bunkered there, trapped by your own tee
shot."

"Mercy!" but the cry halted, inar-
ticulate upon the parched lips.

"A lethal agent! the swiftest and
the surest of them all!" shouted the
Colonel.

An attendant stepped forward with

an oblong package done up in whity-brown wrapping-paper, and *Col. Bogey*, snatching it from his hand, began to tear off the wrappers.

"Ha! ha! One dose of this, and I can promise you that you will never play golf again. Ah! you will, eh?"

Morgan Gordon, in his agony, was straining hard at his bonds. They cracked and partially gave way. But the *Colonel* was kneeling upon his breast, and Gordon was at a tremendous disadvantage. Even as he caught at his enemy's throat the heavy hand descended.

"Take that, and be bunkered to you!" yelled the infuriated *Colonel*. The whity-brown parcel fell with crushing weight upon his temple, and Morgan Gordon knew no more.

* * * *

The morning sunshine was streaming through the open window, and for some minutes Morgan Gordon lay perfectly still in the utter exhaustion that is wont to follow upon sudden relief from overwhelming physical and mental strain. Then, as his mind grew clearer, the ugly horror of that last fearful struggle began to pass away, and he drew a long breath of intense thankfulness. So it had only been a dream—only that, and nothing more. The clock struck eight, and the familiar sound brought with it a fresh accession of confidence and relief. He was himself again, the terrors of the night were a thing of the past, unsubstantial shadows that had fled away before the honest morning light. He jumped out of bed and laughed aloud. "Golficide, indeed! what a roaring farce it had been. How could he even in a nightmare—" The words froze upon his lips, and he stood motionless, staring stupidly at an object lying upon his writing-desk.

It was an oblong package done up in whity-brown wrapping paper.

*   *   *   *

An hour later Morgan Gordon sat in the Townley drawing-room, awaiting the issue of his fate. He had hoped to come bearing with him the first-fruits of a great renunciation, but, since the gods had willed it otherwise, he must needs be content. But how about Alice Townley? She had made her conditions; would she be satisfied with anything short of their literal fulfilment? And so Morgan Gordon waited.

She stood before him, exceeding fair in her glorious young womanhood. A red spot burned on either cheek, her lips were parted expectantly, but she waited for him to speak. He rose and faced her steadily.

"I could not do it," he said, briefly.

The offended majesty of the woman scorned possessed her wholly. "So you prefer your golf; I thought that it would be that way." Her eyes blazed. "*Your* golf! I am humiliated, indeed."

Gordon winced at that, but he would make one final appeal. "But you do not, cannot understand. This golfi-

cide, of which we have spoken so lightly, is an act that means something
more—"

"Than my love."

The challenge of that look was as the
clash of rapiers in salute. And then,
suddenly, and with a great thrill, Morgan Gordon knew his own heart. What!
had he been seeking to bargain for
this precious thing that men call love?
When one has found an inestimable
jewel in the great world-bazaar, dare he
stop to haggle over its price? can he
hope to cheapen it, except to his own
irretrievable loss? Quick! he must not
hesitate now.

"No; not more than that, not more
than your love." He took from his
pocket the oblong package, still in its
whity-brown wrapper. He smiled as
he held it out for her to see. Miss
Townley drew back; there was something in this that she did not like.

"I hope that you are not going to do
anything foolish." She spoke with as-

perity, but there was a new note in the cadence of her voice.

"Only golficide. I, at least, went far enough to procure the means to that desirable end. And so, Voila!"

Womanlike, she had repented at the very instant of her triumph. "Put the horrid thing away," she said, pettishly. "It makes me shiver to look at it. And such nonsense, too."

"It is the only way," said Gordon, steadily. He broke the seal of the wrapper, and cut the string that bound it.

"Don't!" and with a wholly instinctive impulse she put out her hand to restrain him.

"Too late!" and as the torn wrapper fluttered to the floor, darkness descended like a veil before Alice Townley's eyes. And Morgan Gordon stood alone, holding in his hand the accursed thing.

It was the Badminton volume on Golf, edited by Horace G. Hutchinson. Fifth edition, fully revised, with new plates and additional reading-matter.

With a firm hand Morgan Gordon turned to the chapter headed "Elementary Instruction," and began to read.

*　　*　　*　　*

It was in the smoking-room of the Marion County Club that I sat with Morgan Gordon and listened to this strange story. He had just returned from his honeymoon, and was as happy as any man can ever hope to be on this old gray earth. When he had finished he looked at me gravely.

"Of course I understand the point you are making," I began, hesitatingly. "Everybody knows that the man who goes in for *Badminton* never plays golf again. There's your golficide all right enough, but isn't there something more? Logically, you are a golficide, and condemned for life to the horrors of the *Pons Asinorum*. But, frankly, you don't impress me that way."

"And quite rightly, too," returned

Gordon, with a hearty chuckle. "As of old, I play a cleek shot wide to the left, and then sneak a brassey around the corner. I haven't been in the bunker once in three weeks."

I confessed my entire inability to take his meaning.

"Simply upon the principle that a man who has taken an *overdose* of morphine doesn't die. I have never told anybody before, but the fact is that I started my career not with golf, but with the exercises and movements recommended in the well-known golfing manuals of Messrs. Everard, Linskill, Forgan, Park, and Sir Walter Simpson. I knew them all long before the Marion County Club was organized, or I had even seen a golf ball. Cut approaches, wrist shots, three-quarter strokes! why, I was accumulating them by the dozen, while you fellows were wasting your time playing matches and making the ball go. With every new book there was a fresh lot of 'em, and you can't imagine the intense fascination that there is in sorting out and classifying the new specimens. You wouldn't believe it, but there are twelve distinct styles for driving, and I've catalogued no fewer than twenty-six approach systems and one hundred and nineteen putting attitudes. Why, my dear boy, there isn't a collection like mine anywhere on earth; the British Museum has repeatedly asked me to name my own price."

Morgan stopped to relight his pipe, but I could only look at him in stupid wonder; words failed me.

"You can therefore imagine," he continued, "the joy I felt when that whity-brown parcel resolved itself into the latest edition of Mr. Hutchinson's *Badminton*. Here was still another game for me to learn, a new style to analyze and dissect and classify; for, curiously enough, I had never seen the *Badminton* volume before. And what a glorious game it is, with its 'slow back,' 'don't

press,' 'keep your eye on the ball'! I
tell you, old man, there's nothing like
it, nothing on earth. Why, even Mrs.
Gordon likes the *Badminton* game, and
she is beginning to play it very well, too.
She was a little suspicious of it at first,
for it does bear some resemblance to
golf, but now that she has tried it she
can easily see the tremendous difference.
Ah! but it was a red-letter day for me
when the devil, or *Col. Bogey*, or the post-
man, or whoever it was, left that whity-
brown package on my writing-table."

I found my voice at last. "I think I
understand it now," I said. "You had
only been playing the 'Golf-Without-a-
Coach' game and Mr. Linskill's game
and Mr. Everard's game and Park's
game, and had never played golf at all."

"Precisely," and Morgan Gordon
beamed with pleasure at my acuteness.

"And consequently, not being a golfer, it was impossible for you to commit
golficide, even with the aid of *Badminton*."

"Right you are, my boy. Naturally it follows that I can never now hope to be a golfer—I've been through too much for that. But I like Mr. Hutchinson's *Badminton*, and there's quite enough in it to satisfy my humble ambitions. It's a great thing, moreover, that Mrs. Gordon can enjoy it with me."

A ball crashed through the window, coming from the direction of the seventeenth tee. But what an unearthly slice! Who could have been guilty of it? We rushed to the window and looked over at the teeing-ground. Robinson Brown was standing there with a perplexed expression on his broad, good-humored face.

"It's a pity that some golfers don't know when they are dead and buried," remarked Morgan Gordon. "If you will examine the club copy of *Badminton* you will find Brown's visiting-card at page 86, or thereabouts."

THE HONG-KONG MEDAL.

THE HONG-KONG MEDAL

AT the age of thirty-five but one illusion remained to Henry Alderson, rich, single, and a member in good and regular standing of the Marion County Golf Club. It is hardly necessary to add that it was only in his capacity as a golfer that he lived again in the rose-colored atmosphere of youth, for after the third decade there is no other possible form of self-deception. And it is equally superfluous to remark that he was a very poor golfer, for it is only the duffers at the royal and ancient game who have any leisure for the exercise of the imagination ; the medal-winners are obliged to confine their attention to hitting the

ball clean and to keeping their eye in
for short putts. It was for Henry Alderson and his kind to keep trade brisk
for the ball and club makers, and to
win phenomenal matches against the
redoubtable *Col. Bogey*—a game which
may be magnificent, but which is
certainly not golf. Still, the diversion
was unquestionably a harmless one, and
served to keep him in the open air and
from an overclose application to business. Moreover, it was absolutely certain that the secret of success lay well
within his grasp. A few more days of
practice, the final acquisition of that peculiar turn of the wrist, and then!—
Henry Alderson took a fresh grip on
the familiar lofting-iron that had deceived him so often, and topped another
ball along the turf. Of course the delusion was a hopeless one, but he was
happy in its possession ; and if we who
look on have become wiser in our day
and generation — why, so much the
worse for us.

It was a bright autumn morning, and
Henry Alderson stood at the tee looking at the little red flag that marked
the location of the tenth hole, two hundred and thirty yards away. He had
done fairly well on the outgoing course,
but this hole had always been a stum-
bling-block to him, and that dreadful
double hazard, a scant hundred yards
down the course, looked particularly
savage on this particular morning. On
the left lurked an enormous sand-pit,
which was popularly known as the
"Devil"; and the "Deep Sea," in the
shape of an ice pond, was only a few
yards to the right. Straight between
them lay the path to glory, but for a
"slice" or a "foozle" there remained
only destruction and double figures.

Henry Alderson shuddered as he
looked, and incontinently forgot all
about "slow back." Crack! and the
"gutty" had disappeared beneath the
treacherous waters of the "Deep Sea."
With painful deliberation he teed anoth-

er ball and mentally added two to his score. The club-head swung back, and for one fatal instant his eye wandered from the ball. Bang! and it had gone to the "Devil." Without a word Mr. Alderson took his expensive collection of seventeen clubs from the hands of his caddie and descended into the bunker to meet the Evil One.

It was just fifteen minutes after eleven when Henry Alderson entered upon his ghostly conflict with all the Powers of Darkness. At twenty minutes of twelve the caddie, tired of inaction, crept cautiously to the edge of the bunker and looked in. His master held in his hand a costly patented "driver" that was alleged to be unbreakable. Placing one foot upon the head of the club, he kicked judiciously but with determination at the precise place where the "scare" is whipped to the shaft, and then carefully added the fragments to the heap of broken putters, cleeks, and brasseys that lay before him. The boy, who was wise in his generation, waited for no more, but fled to the club-house.

Henry Alderson came up out of the bunker, took half a dozen new balls from the pocket of his red coat, and deliberately flung them into the "Deep Sea." He then tore his score-card into bits, divested himself of cap and shoes, laid his watch and purse where they would be readily observed, and walked with a firm step to the border of the pond.

Suddenly a quickly moving shadow projected itself over his shoulder, and a cheerful, albeit an unfamiliar, voice hailed him. He turned and saw a stranger standing close beside him. The new-comer was an odd-looking personage, dressed in a semi-clerical suit of rusty black, and carrying an old cotton umbrella and a well-stuffed carpet-bag. He had a keen-looking, smooth-shaven face, with piercing black eyes and an aggressive nose. His complexion was of a curious pallor, as though untouched by wind or sun, but there was nothing in his appearance to indicate either ill-health or decrepitude.

"Possibly a colporteur," thought Henry Alderson. "At any rate, he's no golfer."

"How are you making out?" inquired the stranger, in a tone of polite interest.

It was on the tip of Henry Alderson's tongue to answer, "Fifty-five for nine holes" (his actual score being sixty-three), but at this awful moment, when all the solid realities of life were crumbling away beneath his feet, the lie seemed so small, so pitiful, so mean, and he replied, "Came out in forty-two, but then I lost a shot through having my ball lifted by a dog."

The stranger did not seem to be visibly impressed. "Pooh!" he said, airily; "I should hardly call that golf."

"Perhaps you play yourself," returned Alderson, with what he considered to be a sarcastic inflection.

"Not as a general thing, though I do a round or so occasionally," said the

"'POSSIBLY A COLPORTEUR,' THOUGHT HENRY ALDERSON"

dark gentleman, placidly. Then opening his carpet-bag and taking out a golf-
ball, "It's a very pretty drive from
where we stand. If you will allow me."

He teed the ball, and, with what
seemed to be an almost contemptuous
disregard of all rules for correct driving,
swung against it the crook handle of his
old cotton umbrella. Crack ! and it went
away like a rifle - bullet, close to the
ground for one hundred and twenty
yards, and then, towering upward in the
manner of a rocketing pigeon, caught
the full strength of the breeze for a
hundred yards of further carry, and
dropped dead on the putting - green.
Henry Alderson gasped.

" Shall we walk on ?" said the stranger.

It was a long putt on the green, but
the umbrella was again equal to the occasion. Henry Alderson's eyes sparkled.
This was an umbrella worth having.

" It makes no difference what kind of
a club you use," said the gentleman in
black, apparently reading his thoughts.

"But with this particular make of ball you can accomplish any shot at will, no matter how difficult."

"I'd like to try that kind of ball," said Alderson, eagerly. "Can you give me the maker's address?"

"If you will accept this one, it is entirely at your service."

Henry Alderson stretched out his hand, and then as quickly withdrew it. He remembered now that when the obliging stranger had opened his bag it had appeared to be filled with what looked like legal papers—contracts perhaps—and there was a dreadful significance in the fact that all the signatures were in red. Of course it might have been carmine ink, and probably was, but it looked suspicious.

"If it's a question of signing my name to anything," he faltered, "I don't think that I can accept. I've made it a rule —er—never to go upon anybody's paper. It's—er—business, you know."

The stranger smiled indulgently.

"You are quite right. Nevertheless, you need have no scruples about accepting my gift, for there is no obligation of any kind involved in the transaction."

Henry Alderson trembled, and looked furtively at the dark gentleman's feet, which, as he now observed, were encased in a pair of arctic galoshes some four sizes too large. Clearly there was no definite information to be gained in that quarter ; and as the field that they were in was used as a pasture for cattle, the presence of hoof-marks could mean nothing either way. There was nothing to do but to chance it, and he was not long in making up his mind. He took the ball and stowed it away in his pocket.

The stranger nodded approvingly. "I think that I may congratulate you in advance upon your success in winning the club handicap this afternoon."

"But suppose that I lose the ball?"

said Alderson, with a sudden accession of doubtfulness.

"Impossible. If your caddie has been negligent, you have only to whistle, and the ball will keep on answering ' Here ' until you come up with it. And, moreover, it is indestructible."

" It makes no difference what club I use ?"

" None whatever. If you care to, you can drive that ball two hundred yards with a feather bolster."

"I shall endeavor to do so," laughed Alderson. " You won't—er—come and have a bite of luncheon with me ?"

"Not to-day," said the stranger, politely. " But we shall probably meet again. Good luck to you, and may your success end only with the winning of the Hong-Kong Medal."

The two men bowed, and the dark gentleman walked off. He went to the edge of the " Devil " sand - bunker, marched straight into it, and disappeared. Moved by a sudden impulse, Henry Alderson followed and looked in. There was nothing to be seen, but he thought that he could detect a slight trace of sulphur in the air. However, one may be easily deceived in such matters.

As Henry Alderson trudged back to the club-house it seemed as though the events of the last half-hour had been nothing more than the disordered fancies of a noon-day nightmare. But there was the ball in his hand, the tangible evidence of what had happened. And, after all, the bargain had been entirely in his favor. Whoever the dark gentleman may have been, and Henry Alderson shuddered as he reflected upon one unholy possibility, he was certainly no business man. The wonderful ball was in his, Henry Alderson's, possession, and his chances of eternal salvation were as good as ever.

"Somebody has been stupid," chuckled Mr. Alderson to himself as he entered the grill-room of the club and took up the luncheon card.

The handicap match had been put
down for three o'clock. It was a monthly affair, and the winner had the proud
distinction of wearing a silver cross for
the following period of thirty days. It
was a coveted honor, but of course not
to be compared with the Hong - Kong
Medal, which was always played for at
the end of the golfing year. No one
knew why it was called the Hong-Kong
Medal, and it was certain that its donor
had never in his life been out of the Middle States. But the appellation seemed
to chime in with the somewhat fanciful
phraseology that prevails in all things
pertaining to golf, and it possessed a
sonorous clang tint that was suggestive
of tomtoms and barbaric victories.

It is needless to say that Henry Alderson invariably entered all the club
competitions, and as invariably came
out at the bottom of the list. And yet
no one had worked harder to insure
success. He was absolutely saturated
with the theory and literature of golf,

and could rattle off the roster of open and amateur champions with the fluency of a prize Sunday-school scholar reciting the names of the kings of Judah and Israel. He neglected nothing in the way of precept or practice, and when the club champion got married he had even thought of following his example for its possible effect upon his game. But when he ventured to propose the expedient to Miss Kitty Crake he met with a decided rebuff.

"I shall never," said Miss Crake, "marry a man who is not on the scratch list. When you have won the Hong-Kong Medal, why then we shall see."

Of course, such an answer could be nothing less than the most absolute of refusals. Even in his wildest dreams he had never hoped to come in better than fourth in the monthly handicaps, and that too with an allowance of thirty-six strokes. It is true that there were other young ladies who might have accepted a less heroic standard of excellence than

the winning of the Hong - Kong, but
Henry Alderson felt that the matri-
monial experiment was not worth trying unless Kitty Crake could be induced
to take part in it. And so there the
matter rested.

When Mr. Alderson stepped to the
teeing - ground that afternoon for his
first drive he felt unaccountably cool
and collected, in spite of the fact that
Miss Crake stood in the very forefront
of the "gallery." It was one hundred
and seventy - seven yards to the first
hole, and he usually "hooked" his ball
into the "Punch - bowl" hollow at the
left, or else feebly topped it along the
ground in the one consuming desire to
get away from the spectators. But to-
day there should be another tale to
tell. For an instant he thought of di-
recting the magic ball to land upon the
putting-green dead at the hole, but he
reflected that such a phemonenal stroke
would undoubtedly be put down as a
fluke. It was the part of wisdom to go

quietly, and so he picked out a spot some twenty yards short of the green, but in good line, and affording a generous "lie."

As he lifted his club and swung through he was uncomfortably conscious of having transgressed at least eighteen out of the twenty-three cardinal precepts for correct driving, but already the ball was on its way, and, amidst a hearty burst of applause, led, as he could see, by Kitty Crake, it fell precisely as he had determined. A skilful approach laid him dead, and the hole was his in three. A subdued buzz ran around the circle of the "gallery," and everybody bent forward to watch his second drive across the "Punch-bowl." Straight over the yawning hollow flew the ball, and the crowd clapped again; but the play was now too far away to watch, and there were others ready to drive off. Henry Alderson disappeared in the direction of the "meadow" hole, and Miss Crake went to the club-house piazza to make tea. "Poor fellow," she thought, "his foozling will be all the worse when it does come."

It was a very successful tournament, and Henry Alderson won it by the credible score of eighty net. He blushed as the President handed him the silver cross, but the spectators clapped vigorously; for he had always been a good fellow, albeit a bad golfer, and his victory was a popular one.

"Splendid!" said Miss Kitty Crake, and Henry Alderson ascended forthwith into the seventh heaven.

During the month that followed there were some tremendous surprises in store for the record-holders. Three days after the handicap Alderson did the course in eighty-two, thereby breaking the amateur record, and that same afternoon he tied the best professional score. The Green Committee promptly reduced him to the scratch list, and there was some informal talk of sending him to represent the club at the National Amateur meeting. Montague, the holder of the Hong-Kong Medal for two years running, was visibly uneasy. He began to spend more time on the links, and held surreptitious conversations with Alderson's favorite caddie.

But there was a friend as well as an enemy to keep close watch upon Henry Alderson. There was a change in him that only Kitty Crake noticed at first —a change that both annoyed and alarmed her. The becoming modesty with which he had achieved his first successes had entirely disappeared. Almost imperceptibly he had grown self-sufficient and opinionated, and his attitude towards his fellow-players was at times little short of offensive. He seemed to take an insolent delight in openly flouting the hoary traditions of the game, and in giving the lie direct to each and every venerable truism incrusted in golfing lore. He invariably used a wrong grip; he played with a full swing for all distances, including the shortest of putts, and he never under any circumstances condescended to keep his eye upon the ball. It was maddening to his fellow-golfers, but his scores were a sufficient answer to all remonstrances. Indeed, it may be said that his steadily decreasing averages were beginning to cause the Green Committee considerable uneasiness. For a player to return cards of sixty-four and then fifty-six and then forty-nine seemed to argue unfavorably for the sporting character of the links. Such kind of play was plainly injuring the reputation of the club, and at least the Honorary Secretary was emboldened to hint as much. The very next day Henry Alderson returned a total of eighteen for the full round of holes, and handed it with a mocking smile to the Honorary Secretary himself. This was too much, and Henry Alderson was promptly summoned to appear before the outraged majesty of the Green Committee. But it all ended in smoke. No one could deny that extraordinary scores of a hole in one stroke had been made on several occasions, and in this case it was simply an established phenomenon multiplied by itself eighteen times. "And, gentlemen," concluded Henry Alderson, "I did it all with a wooden putter."

The Green Committee had nothing more to say, but they were plainly dissatisfied, and at once set about putting in some new hazards.

And yet—will it be believed?—Henry Alderson was not a happy man. Egotistical and arrogant as he had become, he yet could not fail to perceive that he had lost immensely in the esteem of his clubmates. Nobody cared to play a match with him; and although at first he had put it down to jealousy, he was gradually forced to admit to himself that the reason lay deeper. Worst of all, Kitty Crake was decidedly cool in her manner towards him. He could not understand it, for his golf was certainly above reproach, and he knew that noth-

ing now could prevent him from winning the Hong-Kong Medal. Once it was
pinned upon his breast he would be in
a position to demand an explanation and
the fulfilment of her promise. But there
was still another reason for his wishing
that the match was over. Strange as it
may appear, the very name of golf had
become an abhorrence to him. And yet
it was not so strange, after all, when one
stops to consider. There is nothing so
tiresome as perfection, and this espe-
cially applies to golf, as possessing an
essentially feminine nature. It is the
capriciousness, the inconstancy, of golf
that makes it a folly so adorable, and
Henry Alderson's game had arrived at
a pitch of intolerable perfection. He
had long ago discovered that the ball
would not be a party to a poor shot.
Goaded into fury by the monotonous
consistency of his play, he had tried the
experiment of ordering the ball into a
bunker, or at least a bad lie. But the
soulless piece of gutta-percha would

havé none of his foozling. It simply would not be denied, and after a few trials Henry Alderson resigned himself to his fate, comforting himself with the reflection that, having won the medal (and Kitty Crake), he would give up golf forever.

The day of the contest for the Hong-Kong Medal had come at last, and all golfdom had assembled to see the battle. A round-robin protesting against the admission of Henry Alderson as a competitor had been presented to the Green Committee, but that autocratic body had decided to ignore the protest. "It will be better," said a wise man, "to let him win rather than to give him a handle for a grievance. Let him take the medal, and then we can settle upon some pretext to expel him from the club. Montague has had detectives on the case, and thinks he can prove that Alderson has been playing tennis within the last two months. That will be sufficient in the eyes of all true golfers."

As it happened, Alderson and Montague were paired for the great event, and, of course, they had the gallery with them. Just before they started Alderson mustered up his courage and walked over to where Kitty Crake was standing. She did not raise her eyes as he approached, and he was obliged to speak twice before he could gain her attention.

" I trust that I am to have the benefit of your good wishes," he said, meaningly.

She looked at him in frosty surprise.

" I don't think that they will help you much." And then, with cutting deliberation, " I devoutly wish that the Hong-Kong Medal had never existed."

" Mr. Montague and Mr. Alderson," called out the referee. The two contestants came forward, and Kitty Crake ostentatiously turned her back as the play began.

In all the annals of the Marion County Golf Club a closer and more exciting match had never been played. Montague was certainly putting up the game of his life; and Alderson, while not showing any phenomenal work, was nevertheless returning a faultless score. Not a mistake had been made on either side, and at the end of the seventeenth hole honors were exactly even. But Montague was visibly breaking under the strain.

When Montague stepped forward to drive for the home hole it was plain that he was very nervous. Twice he tried to tee his ball, but his trembling fingers refused their office, and he was obliged to call upon a caddie for assistance. As he came up for the "address" he was deathly pale, and little beads of sweat were standing upon his forehead. The club swung back, and then descended upon the ball, but with a feeble, crooked blow that "sliced" it hopelessly into the bushes. A groan went up. Montague had "cracked," and the match was lost.

Up to this point Henry Alderson had
played as though in a dream. At last
he understood — those cold, stinging
words of Kitty Crake could have but
one meaning. *She did not wish him to
win!* It was only too plain that she
had never loved him, and that she re-
gretted her idle words about the winning
of the medal and the promise that they
implied. What was he to do?

One thing was certain : he had no
chance, in any event, with Kitty Crake.
Of course he might go on and win the
medal, and then humiliate her by con-
temptuously refusing to press his claim ;
but the revenge was an unmanly one,
and he could not bring himself to adopt
it. Again, he might withdraw, and so
give the prize to Montague. He knew
that the latter was desperately anxious
to retain possession of the trophy. It
was the pride, the joy, the treasure, of
his otherwise empty life. The Montague infants had all cut their teeth upon
the medal's firm and glittering edge. It

was the family fetich; the one thing
that distinguished them from the common herd of their neighbors, who lived
in precisely the same pattern of suburban villa, but whose interest in life never rose above the discussion of village
improvements or the election of a ves-
tryman. Henry Alderson hesitated;
his heart grew soft within him. And
yet to give it up after it had cost him
so much!

"Oh yes, a fair enough player, but a
trifle short in his driving."

It was Montague who spoke, and
Henry Alderson felt instinctively that
the remark referred to him. His cheeks
burned as he heard the half-veiled in-
sult that only a golfer can understand
in its full significance, and he incontinently forgot all about his generous
resolution to withdraw. He stepped up
to the tee.

"I dare say I can reach the green in
two," he said, carelessly.

The hole was some four hundred yards

away, and Montague smiled sarcastically. His enemy was about to be delivered into his hands.

"I've done two hundred and forty yards of straight carry," continued Alderson.

"Hym!" coughed Montague.

"And I'd back myself to make it three hundred."

"Why not four?" said Montague.

"Six hundred, if you say so," returned Alderson, hotly.

"Or perhaps out of sight," sneered Montague.

"Off the earth," retorted Alderson.

Montague made no reply, but turned away to hide his satisfaction. Alderson was deliberately going to "press," and every student of the art of golf knows what that implies. But there is nothing more uncertain than a certainty— in golf.

Henry Alderson swung down upon the ball. Shades of St. Rule! but was there ever such a mighty drive? Three hundred yards away, and it was still rising into the blue ether. Another instant and it had passed entirely out of sight, lost in infinite space. The spectators gasped, and Montague turned livid. But stop a bit. Where *was* the ball? The referee looked puzzled, and the caddies stared open-mouthed into the sky. And then in a flash it dawned upon Henry Alderson that his boast had been literally made good. *He had driven his ball off the earth.*

For a moment his heart stood still. With the ball was gone his golfing reputation, and gone forever. Was there anything else for him in life? The answer came in another flash of inspiration. Yes; he was a free man; now he could play golf again—his *own* game. Forgotten was the Hong-Kong Medal; forgotten for the nonce was Kitty Crake herself. The fit was upon him—the berserker rage of the true duffer. He turned to the referee.

"I acknowledge," he said, "the penalty for lost ball, and play a new one."

He teed a ball, an ordinary gutta-per-cha, and, swinging down upon it, made the most bungling of "tops." A roar of laughter went up, and Henry Alderson joined in it, the heartiest of all. He caught Kitty Crake's eye, and she was smiling too. Taking a brassey, he advanced for his second shot, and "missed the globe" twice running. But what a delightful sensation it was!—this was something like golf.

Finally, he succeeded in playing inside of Montague, who followed with a splendidly played iron shot out of the bushes. Alderson drove into a bunker, and noted, with an exquisite thrill of pleasure, that his ball had buried itself completely in the sand. It took him three to get out, and the crowd applauded. He "foozled" a shot into a clump of evergreens, and Kitty Crake clapped her hands. Montague made a phenomenal approach, and landed his ball dead at the hole. Alderson "hooked" one ball, "sliced" another, and banged a third into the flag, securing a lucky "rub." He missed two short putts, and then managed to hit Montague's ball, holing it, and leaving his own outside. The laughter of the "gallery" gods cleft the skies, and the referee stepped forward.

"Mr. Montague eighty strokes, Mr. Alderson ninety - six. Mr. Montague wins the tournament, and retains possession of the Hong-Kong Medal."

Curiously enough, it seemed as though the applause that followed the announcement was intended for Alderson rather than for the victor. Men with whom he had not been on speaking terms for months crowded around him to shake his hand. From being the most unpopular man in the club he had suddenly become a hero. It was incomprehensible. Last of all came up Kitty Crake. The crowd had drifted away, and they were alone. Her eyes were wet and shining, and she held out her hand. He took it, trembling inwardly.

" Well," said she at length, "the match is over: have you nothing to say to me!"

"But—but I lost it," faltered Henry Alderson.

"Exactly; and in so doing you just managed to save yourself. You have evidently no idea how simply intolerable a champion at golf may be."

"Oh, Kitty—" he began; but they were already at the club-house.

After they were married he told her the whole story.

"But there is one thing I never understood," he concluded, thoughtfully. "If it really were the enemy of mankind, he certainly acted very stupidly in not getting my signature in the good old orthodox way. What had he to show for his side of the bargain?"

"Oh, that is plain enough," answered Mrs. Alderson. "So long as pride continues to be one of the seven deadly sins—"

" Well ?"

"Why, the devil is quite justified in feeling cocksure of a medal-winner at golf. Poor Mr. Montague !"

THE OBSESSION OF ROBIN-
SON BROWN

THE OBSESSION OF ROBIN-SON BROWN

WHEN the Marion County Golf Club was first organized, upon the list of charter members appeared the name of Robinson Brown, of the old-established firm of McTavish & Brown, ship chandlers and general dealers in marine stores at No. 6014 Burling Slip. But it must not be rashly inferred from this circumstance that Mr. Brown was a golfer, or that he took any particular interest in the naturalization of the royal and ancient game. On the contrary, being an American of the Americans, and well into his fifth decade, Mr. Brown had long ceased to care for athletic amuse-

ments, either in an active or in a vica-
rious capacity, and he even held some
old - fashioned notions upon Saturday
half-holidays and the propriety of using
public money for the establishment of
municipal playgrounds. He rejoiced
when croquet became obsolete ; he
viewed with disapproval the introduc-
tion and overwhelming popularity of tennis ; he found himself in entire sympathy
with the attitude of his favorite evening
newspaper towards college football, and
he prided himself upon his inability
to distinguish between a base hit and
an error. For exercise he depended
upon walking (by the doctor's orders)
and the Swedish movement cure (also
by the doctor's orders), and he found
amusement and abundant mental re-
laxation in occasional attendance at
trotting matches and in his regular af-
ter-dinner rubber at seven-point whist.
Simple in his tastes and habits, he desired nothing more of To-day than that
it should follow in the comfortable groove

of Yesterday, and, with the disappear-
ance of his waist, he had insensibly lost
the capacity of any emotion unconnect-
ed with cutlets and the state of the
money market. Such, then, was Mr.
Robinson Brown in the year of grace
eighteen hundred and ninety-five.

It may seem at first sight that in join-
ing a golf club Mr. Brown was acting
decidedly at variance with his well-con-
sidered and often - expressed opinions,
but he had been prompted to the step
by several ulterior considerations. In the
first place, he had seen the game played
while on a visit to a country - house at
Southampton, and he was thoroughly
convinced that it had only to be tried
once to be found forever wanting. In
point of hopeless inanity it could not
be improved upon, and Mr. Brown rea-
soned very acutely that its colossal im-
becility could not be better established
than by public exploitation of its claims
to recognition. The statue had only to
be set upon its pedestal for the clay feet

to crumble, and Mr. Brown confidently hoped that in falling it might hit some other things, perhaps the manager of a college football team, or even a young woman on a bicycle.

Secondly, Mr. Brown was heavily interested in the development of the particular suburban section which would be advantageously opened up to public inspection by the establishment of a well-appointed country club, and if he could clear some thousands of dollars by the sale of lots before the boom in golf collapsed, the investment of a hundred or so in stock and dues would manifestly be a good business stroke. And, finally, it would make a pleasant break in the monotonous round of his daily constitutional drive along the Monkton Road to stop for a few moments at the clubhouse and enjoy the mild refreshment of a "Sam Ward" upon its shady piazzas. He had always thought that the town club should maintain a country annex during the summer months, and

the golfing madness, while it lasted,
would at least insure a respectable ar-
ticle of Scotch whiskey. And so the
Marion County Golf Club took to itself
a local habitation and a name, and the
signature of Robinson Brown stood first
upon the roll of incorporators.

It was evident from the start that the
new organization was to be a great success, and, strange as it may appear, it
was the golf that made the club so
popular. Mr. Brown was forced to acknowledge that the interest in the new
game was as profound as it was inexplicable, and it was an extraordinary fact
that the middle-aged members were
even more enthusiastic than the young
people. Mr. Brown, from his corner
seat on the wide, cool piazza, watched
the development of the craze with ever-
increasing astonishment. Respectable
citizens, hard-headed business men,
against whose commercial standing
there had never been a breath of sus-
picion, one after another fell victims to

the fascination of the "green," and the surrender once made was invariably absolute. The conversation in the smoking-room was all of "mashies" and of "patent lofters," of "cuppy lies," and of phenomenal "long puts." The state of the market was of distinctly minor importance to these lunatics so long as the great questions of "stance" and "grip" remained unsettled, and Mr. Brown found to his disgust that the popular bond issue and the attitude of the government towards Venezuela were as nothing compared to the establishment of a new record for the course. He raged inwardly at the senile folly of his former friends, and openly made sarcastic comments upon the appearance of their legs, but all to no avail. The most he could hope for was that the very virulence of the disease might effect a cure, that the craze might be as short-lived as it was furious. But the days slipped away into weeks, and the end was not yet.

Now it happened upon a certain pleasant afternoon that Mr. Brown appeared at the club somewhat earlier than was his wont. He was indulging in the rather unusual luxury of a holiday from business, and, truth to tell, he did not know what to do with it. He was tired of being driven up and down the Monkton Road, so he ordered the coachman to turn in at the club. There were only half a dozen of the members about, and Mr. Brown saw to his disgust that they were all confirmed worshippers of the goddess of Golf. He stalked gloomily down to the teeing-ground to watch the players drive off, and make sarcastic comments as, one after another, the strong men bobbed and scuffled and writhed and scraped in their futile endeavors to render meet obeisance to this new Baal.

The last three players had been waiting to play a " foursome," but the fourth man had failed to put in an appearance and they had decided to play a three-ball match. They were Hardinge, the secretary of the club; Mason, who was an acknowledged power in the whole-sale - grocery world; and Woodhouse, better known as *The Fiend*, from the fact that he took all his meals at the club-house, and was popularly supposed to sleep upon the course while engaged in practice for the monthly medal. Now Hardinge and Mason had been erstwhile bosom friends with Robinson Brown, and it irritated him to see them so completely given over to this senseless in-fatuation. He jeered at Hardinge when he "topped" his drive, and sarcastically suggested "the side of a house" to Ma-son after that gentleman had "missed the globe" five times running and had broken his favorite play - club. The players bore Mr. Brown's badinage with ill-concealed impatience, but Woodhouse was winking expressively, and they re-mained silent.

"Perhaps you'd like to take a hand, Brown," said *The Fiend*, carelessly, as he teed his ball and struck off. "Not a 'foursome,' you know, but just a four-ball game around the short course." And thereupon, with an ingratiating smile, he actually forced a club into Mr. Brown's astonished hands just as a drag full of people rumbled along the drive and pulled up directly in front of the teeing-ground.

It was a very embarrassing position for Mr. Brown, this public discovery of Saul also among the prophets, and his first impulse was to employ the club upon Mr. Woodhouse's impertinent person. But another and sweeter form of revenge instantly presented itself—to surpass by one brilliant and overpowering stroke *The Fiend's* own drive (which was really rather ordinary), and then to scornfully retire from the contest upon the ground that it was too easy to be interesting. Not the shadow of a doubt as to his ability to perform the feat clouded Mr. Brown's mind, and it is therefore not surprising that he even exceeded his own expectations. The ball went off the club with the most perfect accuracy, and actually fell dead at the hole 170 yards away. Mr. Brown's revenge was ready to his hand, but he did not take it ; he could have crushed *The Fiend* with a single word, but he did not say it. Silently, and yet with the air of a man who knows when he has done a good thing, Mr. Brown proceeded to the putting-green and waited majestically for the other players to come up. It is hardly worth while dwelling upon this remarkable inconsistency on Mr. Brown's part. No explanation would be satisfactory to the non-golfing mind, and to that of the golfer none is needed.

As Mr. Brown's ball rested on the very lip of the cup it was impossible for him to foozle the putt, and the hole was his in two—"a record, by Jove !" as Hardinge exultantly proclaimed. Mr. Brown felt impelled to tell exactly how he did it, and he was pleased with the

respectful attention accorded to his re-
marks. "And now whose honor is it?"
concluded Mr. Brown, cheerfully. "You
play straight over that flag, I believe.
Hey there, you boy! Fore!"

Mason managed to draw *The Fiend*
to one side. "What on earth!" he began—

"Sh!" interrupted *The Fiend*, warn-
ingly. "It simply means that I haven't
forgotten what that man Brown once
said about my legs."

Mr. Brown finished the round in very
fair figures for a beginner, and, although
it was growing late, persuaded Woodhouse into taking a turn around the full
eighteen holes. It was long past the
Brown dinner-hour when they had finished, but the new convert did not appear to attach any importance to that
fact. He insisted upon driving *The
Fiend* home, and before they separated
an agreement had been reached for a
meeting at the club the next afternoon.

"And be sure you hunt me up that

address—where I can get a red coat, you know," bawled Mr. Brown, standing up on the back seat of the rapidly receding carriage. *The Fiend* laughed as he entered the house, and the sound was not a pleasant one.

It is a remarkable fact that Mr. Brown bought no less than thirty-seven drivers before finding one whose length and "lie" exactly suited him, and as he broke that one on the very first round he began to have a realizing sense of the exacting nature of the fascination to which he had yielded himself. Of course the first ambition of every true golfer is to possess an absolutely perfect set of clubs, and Mr. Brown felt very much annoyed at his misfortune. However, his collection of irons was perhaps unequalled in the country. His driving-cleek was a noble instrument, purchased at about its weight in gold from a celebrated professional player whose identity may be thinly disguised, under his familiar sobriquet of "Willie."

It was really a good cleek, and Mr. Brown expected to do wonders with it at the next monthly handicap. For practice work he bought several others exactly like it in appearance, and unfortunately got the lot all mixed up through the stupidity of a caddie. This was even more disheartening than the loss of his driver, and, although the professional was called in and commissioned to pick out the masterpiece, Mr. Brown never felt quite sure that the lost treasure had been recovered. Assuredly the cleek did not play the same as when "Willie" had used it in establishing a new record for the course, and Mr. Brown felt vaguely that he had been swindled. There could be no doubt, though, about his wooden putter, a monstrosity that bore the name of "Philp," and which was guaranteed to have once belonged to Allan Robertson himself. It was a glorious weapon, and as Mr. Brown invariably used an iron putter he never lost his confidence in the playing qualities of his treasured antique.

All this, of course, cost more or less money, and the size of the club-maker's bill rather startled Mr. Brown when it was presented at the end of the month. "Though, after all," he thought to himself, "I should probably have spent as much in 'Sam Wards' and been none the better for them." Of course the unhappy man had entirely ignored the fact that his consumption of "Scotch and soda" was increasing in inverse ratio to his abstinence from other forms of liquid refreshment ; but the delusion is not an uncommon one among the fraternity of golfers, and nothing is so misleading as statistics, with the possible exception of "Scotch and soda" itself.

One afternoon, about ten days after Mr. Brown's conversion, Mrs. Brown was surprised to receive an early morning call from Mr. McTavish, the senior partner in the firm. On descending to the drawing-room she found that gentleman in a state of unusual excitement, and it was with some difficulty that she finally gathered that he had come to inquire as to the whereabouts of Mr. Brown. On her informing him that Mr. Brown had taken a day off, and was spending it upon the golf course, Mr. McTavish drew a long breath of relief, but it was evident that he was both surprised and annoyed. It appeared that Mr. Brown had given no intimation of his intended absence, and as he held the combination of the safe it had been impossible to transact any business at the office. In this emergency Mr. McTavish had taken the first train out to Lauriston to find out what was the matter. "And I was prepared, madam, for the worst," he concluded, gravely.

"Apoplexy, perhaps," hazarded Mrs. Brown, smilingly.

"Or Canada," retorted Mr. McTavish. Well, of course, it was unjustifiable,

this insinuation on the part of the senior partner, but it must be remembered
that Mr. McTavish was a very dignified
old gentleman, with a tendency to suppressed gout, and Mr. Brown's derelic-
tion had put him to a great deal of
bodily inconvenience and mental dis-
comfort. It was annoying to find that
all this pother had been caused by a
ridiculous game of golf, and Mr. Mc-
Tavish considered that he did well to
be angry. Nevertheless, Mrs. Brown resented the imputation, and some warm
words passed.

"I shouldn't have cared," said Mr.
McTavish, bitterly, "if Brown had
broken his leg or had been killed on the
railroad—that would have been *some*
excuse."

"Oh, indeed!" put in Mrs. Brown.

"But to find him playing golf with
the market liable to go to pieces at any
moment—I don't know what I can say
to *that*, I really don't." And Mr. Mc-
Tavish stopped short, in the conscious-

ness that the English language was entirely unequal to the due expression of
his feelings.

"Perhaps you've said quite enough
already," remarked Mrs. Brown, icily;
"but I don't know what you are to do
about it unless you go in for golf yourself."

"I go in for golf!" gasped Mr. Mc-
Tavish.

"Why not? It would help you to understand Mr. Brown's position and be
an excellent thing for your health. Mr.
Brown was never better than since he
took to golf. It keeps him in the open
air, he has a splendid appetite, an excellent temper, and he hardly ever
drinks a 'Sam Ward' nowadays, a point
which some other people might do well
to bear in mind at this hour in the
morning."

And then Mrs. Brown gathered up
her skirts and sailed majestically out of
the room, leaving Mr. McTavish to don
the conversational cap at his leisure.

Whereupon the senior partner hurried back to town and immediately sent for his lawyer and a safe expert.

When Brown came home that night, fresh from a glorious victory over *The Fiend*, Mrs. Brown told him of her visitor and his extraordinary behavior. Mr. Brown only smiled at the prejudices and narrow - mindedness of the non-golfing class, and went out on the lawn to practise up his " approaching."

It must be confessed, however, that as time went on Mrs. Brown was not wholly satisfied with Mr. Brown's attitude towards all things outside of golf. She smiled indulgently at his fancy of taking a cleek to church in lieu of a walking-stick, but she frowned when she discovered that he had laid out a course of short holes among the flower-beds, and she was annoyed to see that the front lawn looked as though a " Sir Roger de Coverley " had been performed upon it by a select company of patent harrows and steam-ditchers. It was also very provoking, upon the occasion of a grand dinner - party, that Mr. Brown should have brought up from the city a dozen golf balls instead of the French artichokes that he had been instructed to procure. The cook had done his best, but even a marvellous sauce could not make them go down with the guests, and the chef had given warning the very next day. It was too bad, for he had been a veritable treasure, a real pearl among cooks.

Mrs. Brown finally felt impelled to have a serious conversation with her husband. She pointed out to him the fact that he had not been near the office for a month, and although Mr. McTavish had offered no remonstrance either verbally or otherwise, his very silence was portentous. As Mr. Brown's income was derived solely from his interest in the business, he could not afford to entirely ignore his responsibilities, and, after all, golf was simply an amusement and not the real business of life.

Mr. Brown listened attentively to what Mrs. Brown had to say, and acknowledged frankly that he had been doing wrong. He would go to town, effect a reconciliation with Mr. McTavish, and take up his duties with new zeal and fresh determination. Yes, he certainly would do that—it was the only proper course.

"But when will you go?" urged Mrs. Brown.

"Just as soon as the monthly handicap is over," answered Mr. Brown, firmly.

Mrs. Brown said no more, but she turned away with a sigh, and with an uncomfortable foreboding of what the future might bring forth.

Two or three days after this conversation it happened to be wet, and Mrs. Brown had occasion to go to town. On returning home at evening she was surprised to see the house brilliantly lighted from top to bottom, and on entering she was still further amazed at the sight

that presented itself. All the furniture
from the hall and the rooms opening
into it had been removed from its proper place and piled up here and there in
fantastic heaps. There were dents and
scratches on the polished mahogany,
and Mrs. Brown's face grew rigid as she
saw two or three "stars" in the big
mirror over the library mantel-piece.
There was a heap of wet sand on the
costly Bokhara rug at the far end of
the hall, and, even as she gazed, unable
to believe her own eyes, Mr. Brown appeared from the butler's pantry, attired
in full golfing costume and attended by
Robinson Brown, jr., with his bag of
clubs. Mr. Brown carefully teed his
ball, and, with a loud shout of "fore,"
drove it the whole length of the hall
and drawing-room, to the utter destruction of a unique Sevres vase that was as
the apple of Mrs. Brown's eye. Little
Robinson clapped his hands, and Robinson, sr., proudly announced that his
score was only thirty-six from the first

tee in the third-story bath-room, not at all bad considering that he had been bunkered in the china-closet.

"The china-closet!" repeated Mrs. Brown, mechanically.

"Now then, Robinson," said Mr. Brown, gleefully, "get me another cut-glass tumbler, so that I can hole out. No, never mind, this inkstand will do."

Mrs. Brown, unable to speak or move, sank helplessly upon a fauteuil which had not been needed for bunker-building, and watched Mr. Brown with fascinated eyes as he proceeded to execute an approach shot over a Louis Seize mirror laid face upward on the floor in lieu of a water hazard. Unfortunately the ball fell short and rolled directly on the mirror, forcing Mr. Brown to call for his "president." Mrs. Brown groaned as the niblick crashed into the glass, but Mr. Brown exulted vociferously, for the ball plumped squarely into the inkstand, sending a shower of stygian drops over the lace curtains.

"Forty for the nine holes," announced Mr. Brown as he restored the club to the bag and turned to find himself in what can only be described as the "PRESENCE" of Mrs. Robinson Brown.

Now just what happened during the subsequent interview does not concern us, but the fact remains that early the next morning Mr. Brown started for his office in the city. On the train he took up a daily paper, and was unpleasantly surprised to see among the business announcements a notice of the forthcoming dissolution of the partnership now existing under the firm name of Mc-Tavish & Brown, ship-chandlers and general dealers in marine stores at No. 6014 Burling Slip. Mr. Brown felt in his heart of hearts that Mr. McTavish was amply justified in his action, but he went on in the faint hope of inducing him to reconsider it. But the interview was in vain. The senior partner treated Mr. Brown with dignity and had no reproaches to make. But his resolution was inflexible — the business must be wound up.

Mr. Brown returned home and talked over the situation with Mrs. Brown. It would, of course, take some weeks to adjust all the interests of the firm, and in the meantime they would have little or no income for current expenses. Mrs. Brown suggested sending for her Uncle Henry, who could advise and perhaps assist them in their embarrassing emergency. A wire was accordingly despatched to Mrs. Brown's Uncle Henry, and that gentleman was good enough to respond to the appeal by taking the first train out to Lauriston. As he stepped out of the carriage at the Brown mansion a small, white, round, and excessively hard object struck him squarely on the leg, causing him several moments of exquisite anguish. Mr. Brown, who had been experimenting behind the ice-house with a new driver, was profuse in his apologies, but Mrs. Brown's Uncle Henry refused to enter the house and took the first train back to town.

It was some three days before Mrs. Brown could bring herself to speak calmly to Mr. Brown, but she could not forget that she had once loved him and was still his wife. She forgave him fully and freely, but it was hard to feel that Mr. Brown's inconsiderate act had not only deprived them of the hope of immediate assistance, but would in all probability have a serious effect upon the ultimate disposition of the old gentleman's property.

" It all will go to the Asylum for Aged Gold-beaters," said Mrs. Brown, sadly, and Robinson Brown ground his teeth in silence.

Still, Mrs. Brown did not wholly despair of the future, for Mr. Brown had now signed a solemn pledge of total abstinence from golf. There was yet time for him to retrieve his past errors, and Mrs. Brown helped him like the true woman that she was. She gave up nearly all of her time to playing parlor croquet and Halma with Mr. Brown, and, although these simple amusements were but melancholy substitutes for the royal game, yet they afforded some temporary relief from the awful craving that at times nearly overpowered him. And as the days went by Mrs. Brown felt almost hopeful again. It was now three weeks since Mr. Brown had touched a golf-club, and the legal formalities of winding up the business were fast drawing to completion. In another fortnight Mr. Brown would have his money at his disposal and be ready for a fresh start in life. They would move to some Western city where there was no club and where public golf was not allowed. Surely there must be some such haven of refuge, and once more removed from the possibility of temptation, all would be well again. Mrs. Brown's face grew hopeful and tender as the vision rose before her. Ah! how happy they would be!

It was drawing on to luncheon-time, and Mrs. Brown, dismissing her day-dream with a half-smile at her girlish romanticism, stepped out into the hall on her way to the dining-room. As she passed the closet where Mr. Brown's clubs and golfing paraphernalia were stored she saw with a sickening sense of fear that the lock had been forced and that the closet was empty. Hardly breathing, she flew out upon the lawn. Gracious heavens! Her worst fears were indeed realized, for there stood Mr. Brown, wearing his awful golf face and sur-rounded by his entire collection of eighty-seven clubs and a dozen careful-ly teed balls. And as she stood with aching heart and tear-dimmed eyes, she saw by his side Robinson, jr., the eldest boy and the pride and joy of the Brown family. She heard Mr. Brown speaking to him in a coaxing tone, as in a dream she saw the besotted, cunning smile with which he sought to force a club into the innocent child's hand.

The wretched man placed a ball in front of the boy and showed him how to grip the club. "And now remember," said Mr. Brown, "slow back! Don't press! Keep your eye on the ba'!"

Mrs. Brown never clearly remembered just how she managed to do it, but in the next instant she had dashed in between father and son, snatched the accursed thing from the child's hand and hurled it far out upon the lawn, farther indeed than Mr. Brown had ever been able to drive a ball.

Husband and wife faced each other.

"Mr. Brown," said Mrs. Brown, "for myself I have nothing to say. But there is no law, human or divine, which can compel me to stand by and see my innocent child deliberately started upon the dreadful road that can end only in 'Walkinshaw's Grave.' There shall be no open scandal, but I shall take Robinson, jr., and the other children and go to my Uncle Henry's by the four train."

Robinson Brown was sober enough now. He turned perfectly white, but his voice was clear and firm.

"You are quite sure, Mary, that you are justified in taking this step?"

"Yes, quite sure."

"And there is nothing, absolutely nothing, that I can do or say to alter your determination?"

He spoke quietly, but there was that note of stress in his voice that betrayed the strong man's agony.

"Absolutely nothing."

"Very well," said Robinson Brown. "While you are packing, I think I'll go and work up my putting a bit."

For the sequel to this remarkable story I am indebted to *The Fiend*, who told it the other night to a select company of the "Old Guard" in the smoking-room of the club.

"As you all know," he began, "it was useless to try and straighten out the tangle, for after Mrs. Brown's departure poor Brown, relieved of all restraint, entered upon a perfect orgy of golf, and for three weeks the niblick was hardly ever out of his hand. Then he seemed to brace up for a time, but the tone of his system had been so lowered by his long-continued dissipation that the reformation was only temporary, and he soon fell back into his old courses—or, shall I say, links. It was pitiable, and no one realized his condition more acutely than he did himself; but what was there to be done? Poor Brown was absolutely unable to pass a golf club without dropping in for a round or so, and at last he lost all sense of decency and openly frequented public golf courses. The Green Committee felt very sorry for him, and as he had no regular home he was tacitly allowed to take up his quarters in the Great Sahara bunker, just this side of the eleventh hole. He had been accustomed to spend most of his time there anyhow, and I suppose that it seemed familiar and homelike to him.

How he managed to live I don't know.

"Well, one day Brown was in the bunker, as usual, working away with his niblick. He had just missed the ball for the seventeenth consecutive time and was about to say as much,* when the words suddenly died away upon his tongue; a new and peculiar sensation pervaded his entire being; he stood stockstill, astonished and almost terrified. Little by little the dark clouds were rolling back from before his tortured eyes, the crushing weight was being lifted from his aching brain, a heavenly calm was stealing gently over his agonizing soul, his tired muscles were relaxing into peaceful rest, and with a great gulp of unspeakable relief Robinson Brown realized that he was a free man, saved as by fire and at the eleventh hole.

"He bent down and picked off the burrs from his stockings, his heart al-

* Golfing euphemism.

most bursting with its mingled emotions of thankfulness and praise. Then, straightening up, he looked with new eyes upon his surroundings. That awful Great Sahara bunker! What a horrid place it was! How could he have possibly endured its dismal presence throughout all these weary weeks and months? And that wretched ball! What a loathsome-looking object! all hacked and scarred and paintless. Well, if he never got it out, why should he care? *He didn't care!* Ah, the intoxicating ecstasy of that bare thought—HE DIDN'T CARE! With a sudden movement of his heavy heel he ground the ball deep into the soft sand, and turned his back forever upon the Great Sahara bunker.

"Clothed and in his right mind, Robinson Brown quickly made up his mind as to what he should do. It was a hard step to take, but he had sinned and he must take the consequences like a man. Reparation, atonement! at least he could make acknowledgment of his

error. Forgiveness! but forgiveness is
divine.

"Mrs. Brown's Uncle Henry lived at
Rhinebeck, and he could just make the
connection with the Saratoga Express.
As fast as steam could carry him he was
whirled up the river and, arrived at his
destination, took a hack out to Uncle
Henry's place. He hardly dared to
think even for a moment of what was
coming, of what might come. Mrs.
Brown, Mrs. Brown's Uncle Henry,
Horace McTavish—and he who had
been a golfer! For the moment his
heart stood still, he was about to order
the driver to pull up; but he stayed
his hand and the hack rolled on.

"On reaching the gate, Brown dis-
missed the vehicle, intending to steal
quietly up to the house by making a
short-cut across the south lawn. The
grounds were surrounded by a high
evergreen hedge, and as he approached
it he heard voices. His heart leaped
as he recognized Mrs. Brown's well-

remembered tones, and Robinson jr.'s boyish treble. Surely, too, that was Uncle Henry's deep bass, and, most remarkable of all, he could distinguish the unmistakable Doric accents of his old partner, Horace McTavish. There was a moment's silence, and then followed an extraordinary and confused medley of shrieks, laughter, and muttered objurgations. What *could* it mean? Almost suffocating under stress of so many and complex emotions, Robinson Brown noiselessly stepped up to the hedge and looked over.

"*Mrs. Robinson Brown, Uncle Henry, Mr. Horace McTavish, and Robinson Brown, jr., were playing a 'foursome' at golf, and Mrs. Brown's Uncle Henry had just laid Mr. McTavish a stymie.*

"Well, they heard the sound of the fall, Brown being a heavy man, and after some trouble they managed to get him into the house and sent for the resident professional. The latter looked grave at first, but after a short, careful examination of all the symptoms he was enabled to assure Mrs. Brown that the case was by no means hopeless. Hard work and business distractions would be the best remedial agencies, and of course golf in every form must be strictly tabooed. Uncle Henry and McTavish were all kindness and sympathy, and the latter immediately had new partnership papers drawn up and executed. Uncle Henry made his will in Robinson Brown's own presence, and the satisfactory nature of its provisions went far towards restoring the invalid to his wonted spirits. As soon as the Browns could get moved back into their old home, Mr. Brown resumed his daily trips to his office in the city, and from that on his improvement was rapid. Of course Mrs. Brown's care and devotion were unceasing. Nothing that could remind Mr. Brown in any way of golf was allowed about the house, and Mrs. Brown even went so far as to have a red coat, belonging to Robinson, jr., packed away in a tin box and carefully buried at the end of the vegetable garden, where Mr. Brown never went by any possibility. With all that it was a long, hard struggle, and at times Mrs. Brown felt almost discouraged. For months Mr. Brown was obliged to drive to the railway station by a roundabout and inconvenient route in order to avoid passing by the golf club-grounds, and he fainted dead away on the train one day when a friend, carrying a newly purchased cleek, happened to enter the car and thoughtlessly took a seat beside him. But the day of deliverance was at hand.

"For a week Mr. Brown had secluded himself every evening in his library, and Mrs. Brown was beginning to feel a trifle anxious. All her efforts to penetrate the mystery were in vain. Mr. Brown was preoccupied, uncommunicative, and certainly up to something. Yet he seemed to be cheerful, even hopeful, and there was a new note of tenderness in his voice when he did speak; it was all very perplexing to Mrs. Brown."

"It was Friday evening and Mrs. Brown's birthday. Mr. Brown rose from the dinner-table, but instead of proceeding alone to the library, in accordance with his usual custom, he silently intimated to his wife that she should bear him company. Pale and trembling, Mrs. Brown obeyed. Robinson Brown carefully locked the door, and then taking an odd-looking object from a secret closet, he presented it to Mrs. Brown. She started back affrighted; what was this monstrous implement, with its glittering, hammer-like head and strange, double-handed grip?

"'The Robinson Brown patent pendulum and self-compensating putting-cleek,' said Mr. Brown, proudly, 'and I invented it myself.'"

Finally, the *Man-in-the-Corner* broke the silence:

"Well, and what then?"

"I do not think," answered *The Fiend*, gravely, "that any words of mine could fitly describe the scene that followed. There are some things, sir, that should be sacred even to a golfer."

The *Man - in - the - Corner* fell back abashed; *The Fiend* took a sip of "S. and S.," and then went on: "Ah! but it is a beautiful sight to see Robinson Brown on the links, surrounded by his re-united family, and restored to comfort, happiness, golf, and his own self-respect. He has never succeeded in getting round under 120, even with the aid of the patent putter, but the sum of earthly felicity is not necessarily made up of the material figures of a score-card."

"But I don't see yet—" began the *Man-in-the-Corner*.

"Simple enough," interrupted *The Fiend*. "Robinson Brown had temporarily overgolfed himself."

THE PERIPATETIC HAZARD

THE PERIPATETIC HAZARD

To speak in the same breath of Miss Louie Trevor and of a hazard at golf would seem to be a co-ordination of two very opposite ideas, for Miss Trevor was in all respects a very charming young woman, while there is nothing in the range of vituperation that may not be legitimately applied to a hazard, be it cuppy lie, casual water, or diabolical sand-bunker. And yet there was a figurative sense under which Miss Trevor might properly have been classed among the difficulties of the course. It is bad enough to play before a "gallery" at any time, but when that critical assemblage numbers within itself the one person in the world whose good opinion is worth having, and whose approving smile far outweighs the value of any trumpery medal, why, then the strain may become superhuman ; at any rate, Bob Challis used to find it so ; and he was not the kind of person to be lightly moved by extraneous influences, seeing that he weighed one hundred and seventy pounds and was blessed with a perfect nervous system. It was true, again, that Bob had been in love with Louie Trevor going on now four years, and was very uncertain as to his ultimate chances of success ; but green committees are not accustomed to take difficulties of this nature into account, and the title of this veracious narrative can therefore only be justified by the presentment of the facts in the case. Now, these details are set down succinctly in the minutes of the recording secretary of the club, but that gentleman being of a totally unimaginative turn of mind the bare recital of what occurred by no means tells the story of how Miss Trevor became for the nonce an official hazard of the Marion County golf course. But there was a story there, as the sympathizing lookers-on knew very well, and since it has already been told time and again over the tea-cups on the west piazza, there can be no objection to setting it down in orderly fashion for the edification of all true lovers, and to the eternal discomfiture of Talfourd Jones and his kind.

It was a bright September morning, and as Mr. Robert Challis entered the common room of the Marion County Golf Club he was conscious of an exhilaration of spirit quite in keeping with the favorable weather conditions. And the coincidence was not surprising, seeing that he was only five-and-twenty, was in love for the first time in his life, and had just done the long course in eighty - two — three strokes below the amateur record. Alas! that such perfect happiness should be so evanescent;

its overflowing completeness was but an
evidence of its mortal and transitory
nature. Upon the bulletin-board had
been posted a list of candidates for
membership, and he walked over to look
at it. One name caught his eye.

"Talfourd Jones!" he muttered, dis-
contentedly ; "what the deuce does that
mean ? I thought he was out West
somewhere and clear of Lauriston for
good. Hang it all ! he said so, didn't
he ? It's a beastly shame that a man
shouldn't know his own mind. I'd like
to know just what Mr. Talfourd Jones
is up to now—'pon my word, I would."

But the bulletin-board had no further
information to impart regarding Mr.
Jones and his plans for the future, and
Challis was obliged to betake himself to
the smoking-room, where he sat down
over a Scotch-and-soda to consider the
situation.

Now, no one can be expected to have
a sincere liking for the man who does
everything, from mumble - the - peg up

to steeple-chasing, just a shade better than yourself. Jones was one of those infernally clever fellows who excel without apparent effort in any department of manual skill, and Bob had played second fiddle to him for more years than he cared to remember.

But even apart from that, there was Louie Trevor. Now, their respective relations with that charming young woman had always been somewhat ill-defined, and Miss Trevor had never shown the smallest inclination to arrive at a more definite understanding. As a matter of fact, and if actions mean anything, she rather preferred to aggravate the uncertainty. Finally Jones had left town, but even then Challis felt that he was still being kept at arm's-length. It really seemed as though Jones had played a winning card by going away ; at any rate, his shadowy personality continued to be a disturbing factor in the sentimental equation that Bob was so anxious to work out.

And here he was back again in Lauriston.

But there was still another complication.

When golf was first introduced at Lauriston, Bob Challis tried the game and ran the usual gamut of sarcastic scepticism, amused tolerance, and frantic infatuation. As a matter of fact, he took to golf very readily and soon became one of the club's leading players. It was freely acknowledged that he stood an excellent chance of coming out club champion in the tournament that was to be held in October, and there was one particular reason which impelled him to strain every nerve in order to win that coveted distinction. Louie Trevor was also a golfer, and she took a profound and absorbing interest in the game and in everything pertaining to it. Not that she played well herself, for, indeed, she was a most indifferent performer. What did it profit, in the golfing sense, that in Miss Trevor's eye lay her chief claim to beauty? Soft, tender, and expressive as it was, it was absolutely impossible for her to keep it on the ball. And that exquisitely moulded hand was nevertheless a most fatally incompetent weapon for the wielding of an iron. To see Miss Trevor play golf was a most bewitching and yet withal a most sorrowful spectacle. *C'est magnifique mais ce n'est pas le golf.*

It is human nature that we particularly admire in others the qualities that we know to be wanting in ourselves. Miss Trevor was wildly enthusiastic over Bob Challis—as a golfer. He could not deceive himself as to the character of her flattering interest in his play. It was too clearly impersonal. And yet anything was better than absolute indifference; her undisguised admiration for his golfing prowess might perhaps in time grow into something warmer. At any rate, she expected him to win the Lackawanna Cup at the coming tournament, and had heavily backed him in six-button gloves. Yes, he must, he would, win; everything depended upon his success. To win! and there was the name of Talfourd Jones upon the list of candidates for membership.

It is a tolerably well-established fact that the worst ills of life are those that we encounter in anticipation. To Challis's unbounded surprise, Jones did not seem to take any interest in golf, although elected in due course to all the privileges of the club. And indifference is a much safer attitude than open hostility or compassionate contempt, as Bob knew very well. Jones simply didn't care to play golf, and he certainly knew nothing about the game. He spoke of the clubs as "sticks," pronounced *putt* as though it rhymed with foot, and appeared wholly unable to grapple with the arithmetical subtleties of "one off three" or "four down." He was a duffer, pure and simple.

Now, it was a moral certainty that he would catch the disease in time, but if the inevitable could be staved off for a week or two longer there was no fear of his looming up as a possible rival for the Lackawanna Cup. But how to go about it?

As we all know, in these days of scientific germ theories, there is no surer way of protecting a man against disease than by systematically inoculating him with its attenuated virus. Behold the inspiration! Bob Challis resolved to make Jones golf-proof. He would talk and preach of golf at him until Jones should come to loathe its very name. It should be golf, golf, golf, until the unhappy man should be driven to the awful extremity of golficide—if there be any such surcease for sorrow in the world of cleek and niblick. The treatment should be kept up until Bob had won those gloves for Louie Trevor, and with them the little hand for which they were designed. Miss Trevor, in her feminine capacity, was an inscrutable mystery, but even the strongest chain may have its weak links, and in this case they were golf-links. All of which goes to show that love may sharpen a man's wits, even though it temporarily takes some yards off his driving.

Bob Challis put this ingenious plan of action into immediate execution, and at the end of a week he noticed that Jones was beginning to avoid him. Plainly he was bored by Bob's continual talk of the "shop." This was encouraging, and a day or two after he waylaid Jones and compelled him to take part in a "mixed foursome," a refined mode of torture which might properly come under the head of cruel and unusual forms of punishment. Bob followed up this assault by getting Jones into a corner of the piazza and reading to him from the *Badminton* volume on golf for two mortal hours. Finally, Jones seized his hat and broke away, under pretence of an engagement in town. For three days he did not come near the club, and little by little he took to staying away al-

together. Bob felt that victory was almost within his grasp.

It was the Wednesday before the tournament, and the last day upon which
entries might be made. As Challis
scanned the list posted upon the bulletin he had a comfortable feeling that
no one was likely to press him very
hard. It was another source of satisfaction that Louie Trevor had just returned from Lenox; he was to meet her
at eleven o'clock for a round over the
short course. He might as well have a
pipe while he was waiting, so he walked
into the smoking-room, where he found
Jones yawning over a morning paper.
Somehow his presence gave Challis a
disagreeable shock, but, after all, there
was no occasion for alarm. So he greeted Jones cheerfully and challenged him
to a point-to-point putting contest.
Jones politely but firmly declined, and
Bob thereupon followed him out on the
piazza and began a dissertation upon
the merits of a certain patent in driving-

cleeks. Jones looked bored, and finally said as much. Bob refused to be shaken off, and droned steadily along on the advantages of a "centred" face in keeping the ball straight. He noted with satisfaction that his victim was stealthily reaching for his hat, and proceeded to quote from the authorities.

"I say," broke in Jones, suddenly, "who is that remarkably pretty girl standing at the home hole? I don't remember having seen her here before."

It was Louie Trevor, of course, and Bob reluctantly admitted as much.

"Well," continued Jones, critically, "the ugly duckling has certainly become a swan. *That* Louie Trevor! I believe I'll just stroll over and renew the acquaintance. Eh! What's that? You want me to go and see you try a new driver? Oh, you be hanged, and your *gowf*, too." And Mr. Jones rudely turned his back and strode jauntily away to where Miss Trevor was standing.

Bob tried to follow, but the visible world was spinning about him, and he had to clutch at the piazza railing for support. In an instant he had realized the situation, made terribly plain in those few careless parting words. That significant pronunciation, *gowf;* he knew too well all that it implied. Most of the Marion County members called it *golf*, with a decided leaning on the *l*, and there was a small minority who prided themselves on saying *goff*. But no one ever said *gowf*, a Scoticism that as yet had not ventured south of the Tweed. Could it be possible that Jones was not the duffer that he seemed? And the world spun around again.

A voice at his elbow made him start. Jones was standing at his side and looking particularly animated and cheerful.

"By Jove!" said the perjured one, " but that little Miss Trevor is a ripper, and she's stark mad about the *gowf*. I rather think, old man, that we'll have to have a set-to for the *kudos* of the thing,

though I haven't played since I won the
May Medal at St. Andrew's."

" St. Andrew's at Yonkers?" inquired
Challis, in a dull, dead voice.

" No ; Scotland. I learned the game
there three years ago. Ha, ha! No
wonder you couldn't teach me your
swing." And the hypocritical villain
walked up to the bulletin - board and
wrote in bold characters the name of
Talfourd Jones upon the tournament
list, ending the scrawl with an insuffer-
able flourish.

Now there are men among men, and
after the first shock was over Bob set
his teeth hard and proceeded to look the
situation squarely in the face. Of
course he would play, and play his best
to win, but so far as Louie Trevor was
concerned he must now take his chances
as a man and not as a golfer. He
would not even condescend to expose
Jones's treachery, although by so doing
he might score a point. And, after all,
golf, despite its undoubted merits as an

outdoor sport, was not necessarily a lasting bond of union or a sure basis of conjugal happiness. Supposing that Louie Trevor actually married him on the strength of his game, might she not have reason to regret her action if he chanced to go off in his driving? There was even the possibility of his becoming permanently disabled. What if he lost an arm in a railway smash-up? No! a thousand times no! He would win her if he could, but it should be his heart and not the Lackawanna Cup that he would offer for her acceptance. As for the latter, let the best man take it.

There being a large field of entries, the tournament for the cup was started on Thursday, with the idea that the finals should take place on Saturday afternoon. By the chance of the drawing it fell out that Jones and Challis were in separate divisions, and, as luck would have it, the former was paired with all the incorrigible duffers in the club.

Challis won his first and second rounds by steady work, and succeeded in pulling off his semi-finals by defeating Egerton, the club captain, in a brilliantly played match. Jones still refused to show his hand, and won his games by narrow margins, thereby leading the spectators to believe that he would be an easy mark for Challis in the finals. There was no particular reason for these underhand manœuvres, unless the tortuous mind of Mr. Jones considered that his final triumph would be thereby rendered more brilliant and spectacular. Bob may have understood, but he made no sign.

Greatly to the surprise of all, the final match turned out to be a very even fight. Bob was playing the game of his life, and it was such good golf that Jones had some difficulty in keeping up with the pace. At the finish of the first round of eighteen holes Challis was one up, and the graduate of St. Andrew's was beginning to look anxious.

The "gallery" wondered and applauded, and Miss Trevor was quite beside herself with excitement. It was a ding-dong battle for the next nine holes, and when the contestants started on the last quarter the game was square. Of the next eight holes both men won three, the remaining two being halved, and the score was still even. Challis had the honor at the thirty-sixth hole, and he drove a beautiful low ball that left him in a good position some sixty yards short of the hole. Jones topped his ball on the drive, but, recovering his nerve, made a fine brassey shot that sent his ball flying far and sure. It fell just behind Bob's ball, and Jones was obliged to play "two more," the third stroke laying him dead at the hole. He was sure to be down in four, while Bob was sixty yards away with two strokes to spare. The ball was lying fair, and Bob, taking his "iron," looked up to measure the distance. Now it was all against the rules, but Louie Trevor had some-

how managed to elude the vigilance of
the rope-holder, and was standing a little to his right and some ten yards
ahead of the ball. Bob saw her as he
looked up, and for a moment a mist
seemed to fill his eyes and his pulse
bounded wildly. He felt a jangle at his
nerves that up to this time had been
steady as a rock, but already the club-
head had swung back for the stroke.
Down came the flashing iron with an in-
drawing cut, and the ball, sliced beyond
repair, rose into the air with a gentle
curve directly towards Miss Trevor. Instinctively she put out her hands, and,
mirabile dictu, the ball settled quietly
in them. Incredible, perhaps, but there
are the minutes of the recording secretary; a miracle if you please, but remember that Louie Trevor was an angel.

There was a buzz of "Ohs!" and
"Ahs!" a babel of exclamations and surprised remonstrances, but Miss Trevor
stood motionless as a graven image,
with the ball still in her hand.

"Put it down!" "It's a rub of the green!" "It can't be played at all!" "He loses stroke and distance!" arose in contradictory clamor about the ears of the unfortunate referee, and still Miss Trevor, with white cheeks and close-pursed lips, held the unlucky ball. And then, moved by some inexplicable influence, everybody stopped short and waited for the referee to speak. But it was Talfourd Jones who broke the silence. He spoke coolly and distinctly:

"I think, Mr. Referee, that the question can only be settled under the St. Andrew's Rules for Match Play, and according to number twenty-two:

"'Whatever happens by accident to a ball *in motion*, such as its being deflected or stopped by any agency outside of the match, ... is a "rub of the green," and the ball shall be played from *where it lies*.'

"And also number twenty-nine:

"'A ball must be played *wherever it lies* or the hole be given up.'"

The referee looked puzzled.

"And that means—?"

"That Mr. Challis must play the ball out of Miss Trevor's hands or lose the match," said Mr. Jones, calmly.

There was another buzz from the "gallery" quite impossible to set down in type, since no printer's case could possibly stand the strain upon the box containing the exclamation-points. Of course, Jones's motive in making the point was perfectly clear. If the strict wording of the rule were adhered to, Bob would have to make a pretence at a stroke to get the ball from Miss Trevor's hand to the ground. That would count as his third shot and would leave his ball still sixty yards short of the green, while his adversary's lay dead at the hole. There was not one chance in ten thousand that Bob, in playing the "like," could hole out and so halve the match, and to win it was of course impossible.

"Refer it to the Green Committee,"

suggested Egerton, the captain of the club.

The referee looked relieved, and Bob was about to assent to this reasonable proposition when he again caught Miss Trevor's eye, and to his amazement it expressed a decided negative.

"Well, Mr. Challis?" said the referee, and this time Miss Trevor distinctly shook her head.

"I waive my right of appeal," said Bob, firmly.

Miss Trevor smiled approvingly, and so did Jones.

"Then the ball must be played as the rules provide, Mr. Challis having declined to appeal. Is that clearly understood?"

Both Jones and Challis nodded, and the referee ordered play. Bob stepped forward, but already Miss Trevor had turned and was calmly walking away in the direction of the eighteenth putting-green.

"Hey, there!" shouted Jones, forgetting his manners in his surprise. "I mean, I beg your pardon, but you mustn't do that."

Miss Trevor stopped and looked at him coolly. "Mustn't do what?"

"Why, you're carrying the ball away with you, and it's in a hazard."

"Precisely; and it is still there," said Miss Trevor, opening her hand and showing the ball lying snugly in its pretty, pink palm.

"But you're the hazard yourself," contended Mr. Jones, angrily; "officially declared and accepted as such by both parties to the match. You must obey the rules of the game."

"I don't know of anything in the rules, Mr. Jones, providing for the personal behavior of the hazards, so long as they keep safely what is intrusted to their care. I happen to be a peripatetic hazard, and I shall go where I please." And thereupon Miss Trevor walked on towards the hole.

"I protest!" said Jones, wildly. "I appeal to the Green Committee!"

"You both waived your right to appeal the case," said the referee, firmly, "and I must now stick to the strict interpretation of the rules. To interfere with a hazard would be a distinct violation of fundamental principles. The only thing we can do is to follow Miss Trevor until she stops and thereby allows the ball to be played."

Wondering and silent, the players and "gallery" moved rapidly forward to the home putting-green, where Miss Trevor was standing close to the hole.

"Take out the flag," said the referee, and it was done. "Now, Mr. Challis."

"One moment, please," said Miss Trevor, stooping down and holding the ball daintily in her fingers and directly over the hole. And then the crowd understood at last, and an irrepressible cheer went up that fairly straightened out the flags.

"Where is Mr. Jones?" asked the referee; but that gentleman had effaced himself. "Play three, Mr. Challis," he continued. Bob touched the ball lightly with his niblick and it dropped into the cup.

"Down in three," announced the referee, calmly. "Mr. Challis wins the match and cup by one up."

There was another outburst of cheers and congratulations, and then, somehow, the crowd melted discreetly away and Bob and Miss Trevor were left standing alone on the field of triumph.

The stars were just beginning to come out as they walked slowly back to the club-house. The evening air was so quiet and still that it startled them when, from the distance, came a confused noise of crashing iron and splintering wood. Bob looked at Miss Trevor inquiringly.

"I rather think," returned that astute young person, demurely, "that it must be Mr. Jones breaking up his clubs."

And so it was.

THE LOST BALL

THE LOST BALL

"SPEAKING of extraordinary happen-
ings at golf," said the *Ancient and Honorable*, reflectively, "there was the great
midnight match between Mayne Rivers and Jimmy Traphagen. And it was
pretty golf, too, in spite of the fact that
it took two men to play it and a woman
to lose it."

There was an instant and expectant
silence in the group around the smoking-room fire, for the *Ancient* was the
oldest member of the Marion County
Golf Club, and his reminiscences always
commanded respectful attention. Even
The Fiend, who was practising stymies
into a ginger-ale tumbler, looked up inquiringly.

"I fancy that it was before our day,"
spoke up Alderson ; "but if you don't
mind, sir, we'd like to have the story."

"Hear! hear!" seconded the chorus ;
and the *Ancient* smiled, visibly gratified.
He stared introspectively at the fire
where the fragments of Robinson
Brown's last score-card were still smoul-
dering, while Montague woke up the
Man-in-the-Corner, and the neat-handed
Peter quickly interpreted and made
good the measure of Egerton's expressive wink. The circle drew closer together ; the preliminaries were accomplished.

"Now then, sir, if you are ready,"
reported Alderson.

"It was a long, long time ago," began
the *Ancient*, slowly, "but it was a great
match, gentlemen ; we don't see such
golf nowadays, nor for such a stake,
either. But we'll get to the story all
the quicker if we *chercher la femme*
without wasting any more words.

"And a charming creature she was,

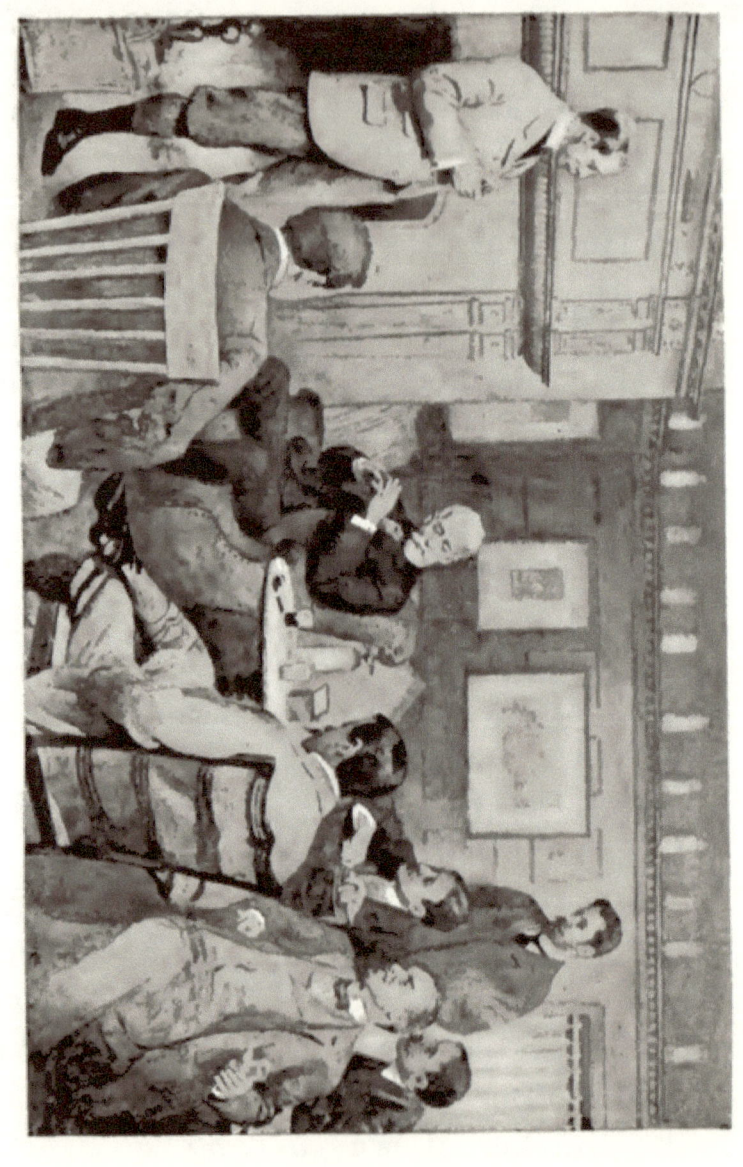

"'IT WAS A LONG, LONG TIME AGO,' BEGAN THE *ANCIENT*"

Mrs. Edna Severn Chase by name, somewhere in the 'truth and twenties,' and a widow without encumbrances. I dare say she's 'fib and forty' now, and perhaps the 'willowy' is inclining a trifle to the 'billowy,' but she's a fine woman yet. I saw her only yesterday driving in the park, and I'm not above confessing that I looked back as she passed. And you would have done the same had you been with me.

"All this, remember, was back in the year one (at the Marion County Club we always used the golfing calendar, and dated everything back to the first national amateur tournament) — in the year one, I say, when golf and Mrs. Chase were the very latest sensations in Lauriston. You should have seen her then, standing at the first tee with the rest of us, fighting for front places in the 'gallery.' Of course she couldn't play golf, but shall I ever forget those frocks? Dear me! it was twenty years ago, and half the members of the club

didn't know the difference between
'one off two' and a 'rub of the green.'

"For all that, we enjoyed our sensations, the foozling that went for golf
and the always fascinating society of
Mrs. Edna Severn Chase ; Mayne Rivers, in particular, and also Jimmy Traphagen—good fellows, both of them, and
golfers too, if you'll believe it, of twenty
years ago. It used to be neck and neck
between them for the possession of the
Hong-Kong Medal ; first one would win
it, and then the other, but they remained fast friends through it all—at
least until Mrs. Chase appeared on the
scene.

"It was not that she gave either of
them any marked encouragement ; in
fact, that was just where the trouble
came in. And none of us suspected
that the delightful widow was at the
bottom of the rather strained rivalry
that gradually grew up between them.
Ostensibly they chose to differ along
golfing lines, and the chaffing invari-

ably ended in the making up of some ridiculous match with a pretty stiff stake to back it. Traphagen would play one club against Rivers's bagful, or Rivers would take a handicap of ten strokes and bind himself to get into every recognized hazard on the course. The rest of us used to find this 'gymkhana golf' very good fun, and we never dreamed of the deadly earnestness that lay behind it all.

"Finally the climax came. There had been a discussion in the smoking-room upon the value of good eyesight in golf-playing, and, as usual, Rivers and Traphagen took opposite sides. The talk grew pretty warm, and at last Rivers intimated bluntly that Traphagen's eyesight must be particularly defective in that he never could see where he wasn't wanted. Jimmy retorted in kind, and the upshot was a match between them for two hundred and fifty dollars a side, and to be played at midnight on the coming Thursday, when the moon would

be down. It was to be a match by holes
over the long course, and it was stipu-
lated that no forecaddies were to be em-
ployed. Each man might have a friend
to carry for him and advise him, but
these assistants would be obliged to
keep behind the ball. It was tacitly
understood that sharp practice would
be largely in evidence, though any detected violation of the rules would, of
course, incur the usual penalties. They
asked me to referee, and I consented,
warning each contestant that I should
certainly uphold the rigor of the game,
and should decide each point solely
upon its merits. And so it was ar-
ranged.

"I need hardly say that the real wager
between the two men involved something more than the money that was at
stake. The private understanding was
that the loser should take the money
and use it in buying railway transporta-
tion out of Lauriston and to the farthest
point of the United States for which it

would pay, allowing, of course, for hotel
bills and for the return trip. During
this enforced absence of the loser the
winner would have a clear field with
the fascinating Mrs. Chase, and might
reasonably be expected to bring his un-
hampered suit to a favorable issue. It
was furthermore agreed that the de-
feated contestant should leave Lauriston immediately after the match, without attempting any explanation of his
extraordinary conduct to the fair one in
dispute. It should be the privilege of
the winner to interpret this cruel and
mysterious action on the part of the ab-
sent one to his own best advantage
with the lovely widow, and it would be
strange indeed if he could not succeed
in turning it to good account. For all
practical purposes the loser would be
once and forever out of the running.
Very clever and ingenious reasoning, as
you must admit, but it had one fatal
and unsuspected weakness — the logic
was all from the masculine standpoint ;

Mrs. Edna Severn Chase, in her feminine capacity, had been entirely overlooked by Messrs. Rivers and Traphagen.

"Now don't ask me to explain how
she came to know all about it—that is
a prerogative of her sex, involving psy-
chology and telepathy and a lot of other
things which lie quite outside of match
play at golf, and are therefore incomprehensible to the masculine mind. It
is enough to say that she did know, and
that she took her measures accordingly,
as we shall see. The rest of us accepted
the match on its exoteric side, and went
in simply for the fun of the thing.
Dick Edwards opened a book for the
accommodation of the sporting element,
and the midnight match quickly became
the sole and all-absorbing topic of conversation.

"Thursday night came, and it was
a dark one, sure enough. Not a star
was visible, the sky was overcast with
lowering clouds, and as one stood at the

tee it was like looking into a bag of black cats. Both principals were on the ground early, and each appeared quietly confident of success. Of course, Mrs. Chase was among the spectators, and just here Rivers scored a point by boldly asking her to caddie for him. Traphagen looked glum at this, but as he had already engaged the services of the resident professional, he could have no objections to offer.

"Midnight struck from the town clock, and I called play. Traphagen won the toss and advanced to the tee. It was a most remarkable-looking ball that he proceeded to address, and the 'gallery' applauded him vigorously—or at least that portion of it who were backing him to win. It was of an ordinary make, but it had been skilfully coated with a phosphorescent paint, so that it glowed all over with a pale, shifty fire, and presented an excellent mark. Jimmy swung through, and away it soared into the gloom, leaving behind

it a luminous track by which its flight
could be easily followed. It fell full
one hundred and seventy yards down
the course, and lay there distinctly visible, an incandescent point that could
not be mistaken or overlooked.

"Rivers did not appear at all discon-
certed by this coup, and immediately
proceeded to drive in turn. But, to the
disappointment of the crowd, there was
nothing unusual about his ball. He
made a tremendous swipe, and it disappeared into the darkness. It sounded
as though the drive had been horri-
bly sliced, but Rivers, who had been in-
tently gazing in the direction of the
hole, quickly announced himself satisfied
as to his ball's whereabouts, and the
procession moved on. 'Think you've
marked it, eh?' said Traphagen, with an
ill-disguised sneer. 'Certainly,' returned
Rivers, promptly; 'it's just ten yards in
front of yours, and on a line with the
hole.'

"Well, we came up with Jimmy's ball,

and Rivers walked on a few steps. 'Here it is,' he called back, and, sure enough, there lay his ball exactly as he had marked it down. Traphagen muttered something about miracles being barred, but there was no going behind the returns, and he was obliged to play the odd. It was some sixty yards to the hole, and his approach shot was wild. Rivers followed, and although nobody could see where the ball went, he confidently proclaimed that it was lying dead at the hole. Jimmy played up, but as the other ball was actually on the rim of the cup, he lost the hole, and Rivers was one up.

"Rivers had the honor, and drove a screecher off into space. I could have sworn that the ball had been pulled clean off the course, but Rivers insisted that he had marked it down in the direct line. Traphagen followed, and it was beautiful to watch his ball whiz through the air like a veritable shooting - star, and fall, a living coal of fire,

into the short grass of the fair green.
There was certainly no shadow of a
doubt as to *its* whereabouts. But, to
the confusion of the sceptics, Rivers's
remarkable powers of vision were again
triumphantly demonstrated. He found
his ball without an instant's hesitation,
and it was full twenty yards inside
of his adversary's. This was truly
magnificent golf. However, Traphagen
made a fine approach, while Rivers foozled. In spite of that, the drive had
taken him to the very edge of the green,
and he was therefore enabled to hole
out in even figures, and so retain his
lead.

"The third hole was a short one, and
both men used their cleeks. 'Right on
the green,' announced Rivers. Traphagen ground his teeth, played wildly,
and followed it up with a worse one.
Score, two up for Rivers ; and I fancied
that Mrs. Chase looked pleased.

"Another short hole followed, and
this time every one could see that Tra-

phagen's ball was lying on the green.
'Where are you?' he inquired of Rivers,
as we walked on. 'Right alongside of
you,' responded that gentleman, coolly.
'Indeed, it was my impression that you
had topped, and, by Jove! I'm right, for
here you are in the bunker.'

"It was Rivers's turn to look discon-
certed, but there was the ball, and he
had to play it. Three or four fruitless
strokes with the niblick, and he lifted,
and gave up the hole. 'I gave you a
chance there,' said Traphagen, as we
walked over to the next tee; 'it would
have been a lost ball but for my stumbling upon it.' Rivers returned thanks,
as in duty bound, but it struck me that
his acknowledgments were distinctly
wanting in heartiness.

"Traphagen got his ball away in fine
style at the next hole, but he had to play
the odd, all the same, for Rivers lay fully forty yards nearer the green. Each
played a brassey, and Rivers again got
the inside place, and, finally, the hole.

He kept up his good work by taking the
sixth and seventh in easy margins, and
his score was now four up. It was truly marvellous, the way in which he managed to keep track of his ball in that
Egyptian darkness. He would bang
away at it with the most perfect uncon-
cern, and with every ounce of power
that he could put into the stroke, but
somehow he always contrived to keep
on the line, and he got in some tremendous carries. It was demon driving
with a vengeance, and perhaps, as Dick
Edwards suggested, he had signed an
unholy compact with the Powers of
Darkness; it certainly seemed as though
the devil himself must be acting as his
forecaddie. But Rivers only laughed at
the innuendo, and so did we. After all,
good eyesight *did* count for something
in golf.

"As for Traphagen, he was playing
in fair form, but he had poor luck in his
lies, and was getting nervous. The
phosphorescent ball was his strong card,

and he had evidently counted upon Rivers's losing several holes through inability to find his ball. To be disappointed in this reasonable expectation was very irritating, and I couldn't help sympathizing with him. And, more than that, I put in some hard thinking.

"At the eighth hole each man had taken three shots, and Traphagen's ball was on the edge of the green. According to Rivers, his ball was also on the green just back of the hole, and he started ahead to verify his assertion. I was standing slightly to one side, and as he passed between me and the crowd I distinctly saw a small white object roll from his trousers leg and settle quietly some fifteen inches from the hole. And then I understood the ingenious nature of the game that he had been playing so successfully under our very noses. It was evident that the rascal had his coat pockets stuffed with balls, and he could drop one wherever he pleased through the simple agency of a hole in his trousers pocket. Of course, on the close range of the putting-greens he was obliged to hole out fairly, but, with one or two odd always in hand, he could easily afford to miss a short putt now and then. No wonder that he had played with such amazing confidence and dash off the tees and through the green. What difference did it make where the ball went to so long as he had another ready to take its place? It was evident that he had never played the same ball twice, excepting on the greens and when bunkered at the third hole. And Traphagen had innocently thought that he was doing him a favor in calling his attention to that latter misfortune. I smiled to recall the surliness with which Rivers had acknowledged the obligation.

"Well, it was clear enough that Rivers had lost an average of at least two balls at every hole, and that instead of being four up he was really seven down. But what was to be done about it? It was none of my business to interfere, and as referee I could only pronounce upon the facts as they were brought before me. Somehow I fancied that Mrs. Chase had also penetrated the mystery, and I tried the experiment of a comprehensive wink in that direction, receiving in return a cold, frosty stare that was not encouraging to confidence. Was it possible that she was really hoodwinked with the rest of the crowd, or could it be that her feelings in the matter were other than I had supposed? I gave it up and turned my attention to the game again ; decidedly, it was getting interesting.

"Now Rivers should have won this eighth hole hands down, but what did he do but miss two short putts, while Traphagen holed out from the edge of the green. The score was now, Rivers three up, with ten to play, and Jimmy was evidently encouraged by his unexpected success in snatching a hole out of the fire. He won the ninth, tenth, and eleventh by good golf, Rivers putting atrociously, and the match was square.

"By this time the 'gallery' had caught on to Mr. Rivers and his little game, and they enjoyed the situation immensely. Every phenomenal shot by Rivers was greeted with a laughing applause that made Jimmy furious, and caused him to miss some of the easiest of chances. Indeed, the match would have been decided at the fifteenth hole had not Rivers showed such lamentable weakness on the putting-greens. This was Traphagen's strong point, and his putting enabled him to win enough holes to square the match again at the seventeenth. Of course, this was the official score. If Traphagen and his caddie, between them, could not see what was perfectly apparent to everybody else, they deserved to lose. A man who was seventeen holes up and didn't know it had no business to be playing golf at all.

" WE ALL DISTINCTLY HEARD THE FATAL SPLASH "

"The old home hole, as some of you may remember, was the longest on the course, over six hundred yards in all, and well protected by hazards. Traphagen had the honor and led off with a moderately good drive. Rivers did not do so well—in fact, we all distinctly heard the fatal splash that indicated that he had pulled into the pond that served as a side hazard to the course. It seemed impossible that Traphagen should not have heard it too, but to my astonishment he made no sign. Such obtuseness was wellnigh incredible. Rivers muttered something about his ball being a hundred and fifty yards or so down the course, and still Traphagen never said a word. Rivers brightened up, and, with a reckless audacity born of success, ventured upon a yet bolder stroke. In such a long hole he had his enemy at his mercy, and he would enjoy the pleasure of playing with him ; he would draw out the agony with the cold-blooded ferocity of the red Indian who has his victim securely at the stake.

"The procession had moved on for about a hundred yards, when Rivers suddenly signalled a halt.

"'I declare,' he said, with admirably feigned coolness, 'I didn't drive quite so far as I thought! Here's my ball now!' and he skilfully dropped one of his extra balls squarely into the most formidable hazard on the course, a bunker which I am ashamed to say was colloquially known as my particular grave. It was a piece of sublime impudence, and I trembled for him, but apparently Traphagen had no suspicions. He and the professional came up and looked carefully at the ball, which lay in the most impracticable of cups. 'Too bad,' said Jimmy, with a genuine note of solicitude in his pleasant voice. Heavens and earth! he was actually sympathizing with that rascal Rivers, and for the moment I was touched—I think we all were. It really *was* too bad; Jimmy was a good fellow, and I felt ashamed of myself and for Rivers. Of course he would own up now—it would be the least that he could do ; and we would enjoy a hearty laugh over the match, and have it declared off.

"But Mr. Rivers did nothing of the kind. With unblushing effrontery he accepted Traphagen's condolences on his hard luck, and proceeded to play the odd. There was a tremendous shower of sand as the niblick ploughed into the ground, but I could see that the ball was still in the bunker. Without an instant's hesitation Rivers buried it in the sand underneath his heel, and announced in a tone of relief that he had made a fairly good shot out of the difficulty, if he did say it himself.

"'Fairly good shot !' echoed the infatuated Traphagen. 'Why, man, it was a beauty, the finest thing I ever saw ! You got out of that hole in great shape ! It was really superb.'

"Well, as I have said before, it was too bad. I never felt so small in my life ;

but Rivers only grinned; it was despicable of him.

"The play went on. Rivers had taken the opportunity of dropping a new ball in a convenient place while Traphagen was playing up, and this time he gave himself a good shot.

"'By Jove! but you are the luckiest beggar!' remarked Traphagen, as he looked at the excellent lie of his adversary's ball. 'Did you ever see anything like that, McPherson?' he continued, beckoning to his caddie to come up.

"'Na doot but it's verra fine gowf,' responded that gentleman, approvingly. 'The mair so that he's no by ordinar wi' the sand-iron, is Mr. Rivers. He'll be keeping his e'e on the ba' fine, I'm thinking.'

"Here Rivers had the audacity to wink at me, but I fell back upon an official non-committalism, and made no response. I thought his attitude distinctly unchivalrous.

"There were several exchanges of

shots after this, for Traphagen made some very poor ones, and Rivers, in pursuance of his cat-and-mouse policy, contented himself with a bare advantage. Of course he continued to perform his wonders with the ball (or rather balls, for it was more like juggling than golf), and after each miracle Traphagen and McPherson made it a point to come up and pass some admiring comment upon his incredible skill and luck. It was all very gentlemanly and sportsmanlike, and I felt sorry that Rivers should be so lost to all sense of decency as to persist in his indefensible course of action. A gentleman would have put his antagonist out of misery as quickly as possible, and even sharp practice in a midnight golf-match may have its limits.

"The score by strokes now stood, Traphagen nine and Rivers six, and both were lying some seventy yards short of the hole. Traphagen, with a nicely calculated iron-shot, laid his ball well up on the green, and indeed within

six inches of the cup. Rivers, out of
pure bravado, had dropped his ball into
a shallow sand bunker, and he was now
to play one off four. With consummate
coolness he took his driver—the driver,
of all clubs!—and banged away. The
ball bounded off a flat stone, cleared
the bunker face, and skimmed like a
swallow low over the turf and straight
for the hole. It was a fool's shot, but a
very lucky one, and of course it had its
due applause.

"'That leaves me three for the hole,
I believe,' said Rivers, jauntily, and as
referee I was bound to assent, although
it did go against the grain.

"Rivers started forward and then
suddenly halted; his face changed; evidently something was wrong. I guessed
the trouble in an instant—his supply of
extra balls was exhausted. He had
played his reckless game just once too
often, and now his folly was about to
cost him hole and match at this the last
moment.

"Of course the Nemesis that had overtaken him was one that he had richly deserved, but such is the inconsistency of human nature that I found myself actually sympathizing with the villain about to be hoist by his own petard. I even felt tempted to help him out of the difficulty by smuggling a spare ball of my own into his hand. But I discovered that I had none with me, and perhaps it was just as well, for the act would have been a most unbecoming one, considering my official position as referee.

"As it turned out, I might have saved my sympathies for a worthier cause; the artful Rivers was by no means at the end of his rope. Suddenly his face cleared and the ring came back to his voice.

"'Ah! there's my ball, just off the farther edge of the green,' he said, in a tone of relief. 'I was afraid that it might have gone on into the hazard.'

"Well, what luck that fellow did have,

to be sure, and how little he really deserved it! I began to sympathize again with Jimmy.

" 'May I ask, Mr. Referee,' continued Rivers, 'that everybody be kept back ten yards from the green, including Mr. Traphagen and his caddie? I can't do myself justice in putting if there is anybody near me.'

" Now of course he had not the shadow of a right to exclude his adversary from the putting-green, and I was about to say as much, when, to my surprise, Traphagen interposed with a courteous assent. Well, whom the gods would destroy they first make mad; and the farce might as well end as quickly as possible. Accordingly, I ordered everybody back, and Rivers walked over to where his ball was supposed to be lying. With careful deliberation he made the address and played. The putter-head swung through, but I would have sworn before a jury of my fellow-golfers that there was no answering click of 'gutty' to iron, nor could I see that the ball was anywhere on the green.

"'Dead at the hole, but it's still my turn to play,' sang out Rivers, as he followed up his imaginary ball. 'Keep back, you people, till I hole out.'

"Well, it was matchless impudence, but it seemed impossible that it could be really successful. Was Traphagen blind or crazy, or must I doubt the evidence of my own senses? Before I could settle the question Rivers made as though he had played a short putt, and announced that he was 'down in nine.'

"There was a lot of hand-clapping from the 'gallery,' and we all pressed forward to the green. Mrs. Chase was in the lead, and before any one could say a word she had walked over to the cup and looked in.

"'Why, there's no ball here,' she said, in a clear, silvery voice; and Rivers turned absolutely green.

"'Eh? you don't say so!' said Tra-

phagen, in a tone of well-affected astonishment. But of course Mrs. Chase
was right, and the cup was really empty.
Poor Rivers! he was the picture of despair; and there stood Mrs. Chase looking at him, with her pretty lips parted
in a quizzical, mocking smile. I never realized before how cruel a lovely
woman may be in her own soft, feminine way. Rivers started to mumble
something about mistaking a fallen leaf
for his ball, but for once even his colossal nerve failed him. He stammered,
grew confused, and ended lamely. It
was really painful.

"'Lost ball is lost hole and match,'
said one of Traphagen's backers, and
Rivers writhed impotently.

"'Your ball may have gone on into
the hazard, old man,' said Traphagen,
kindly. 'Let's have a look for it,' and
he led the way into a dreadful brier
hazard that lay immediately back of the
hole.

"Now this was really very decent of

Jimmy, for he was under no sort of obligation to aid his rival, even at so desperate a juncture. But Jimmy always was a gentleman, and I couldn't help thinking that Rivers must be feeling pretty mean — that is, if he had any sense of decency left in him.

"Well, we ploughed in and through that abominable place, getting ourselves all torn and scratched up, until the five minutes had just about expired. Suddenly Traphagen sang out, 'Here she is!' and we all hurried up to have a look. There lay the little white sphere, half out of sight, and in the most impossible of cuppy lies. I bent down to have a closer look, and there, plainly stamped upon it in red ink, were the letters 'J. T.'

"It didn't take much penetration to see through Jimmy Traphagen's pretended benevolence. He was simply going to torture his enemy in his turn, for the ball was practically unplayable. I changed my opinion of his gentlemanly character at once; this was a low and despicable trick, to which only a cadger could have descended. But there was no use in exposing it. The time was up, and if Rivers did not play this ball his own would have to be adjudged as lost. It was a desperate chance, but it was his only one.

"'Of course those two putts of mine don't count,' said Rivers, coolly. 'There can't be any shot when there isn't any ball upon which to play. They were only for practice.'

"Indeed! but this put quite another face on the matter! If those inutile strokes were not to be counted, the score would stand, Traphagen ten and Rivers seven; and the latter, with three to spare, might easily manage to get the ball out of the hazard, and halve, if not win, the hole. Traphagen looked thunderstruck, and Rivers smiled in quiet triumph. I was disgusted with Rivers; this sort of thing was for sea-lawyers rather than for golfers. But the argument was plausible.

"'According to Rule 4, any move-ment of the club which is *intended* to strike the ball is a stroke.' It was Mrs. Chase who spoke, and the silence was profound. 'It makes no difference,' she went on, 'that the ball in question is one inch or a mile away from the play-er. Mr. Rivers's intention was clearly evident, and the strokes must stand.'

"It was a Portia come to judgment, and we all gasped. I could not look at Rivers. I felt that this last blow must have completely crushed him. There could no longer be any question as to the direction in which the fair widow's sympathies leaned : Traphagen was un-doubtedly the favored man.

"But the reasoning was incontroverti-ble, and I gave my decision in accord-ance with it. 'The strokes must stand : Traphagen ten and Rivers nine.' The latter had still one for the hole and match (for Traphagen was not yet down), but the chance was of the slim-mest. Rivers's ball, as I have said, was twenty yards from the green, and it looked as though nothing short of a dynamite cartridge could dislodge it. Perhaps, if fortune favored him, he might possibly play out to the edge of the green, and then with a long and lucky putt for a half—but oh, those ifs!

"Well, I couldn't help admiring Rivers as he pulled himself together for this last forlorn hope. He was indeed a man among men, and would die game.

"His face was firm and set as he took his stance and played. *Mirabile dictu!* the ball popped up out of that hopeless pocket, sailed in a gentle curve to the green, ran over it to the hole, and disappeared down the cup. It was the one shot out of a thousand years of golf, and, as though moved by a common impulse of reverence, every man pulled off his hat and bowed his head in silence. Rivers was down in ten, winning match and hole by one stroke. The eighth wonder of the world had actually occurred right here on the home green of the Marion County Golf Club. It was intoxicating, miraculous, sublime.

"It was Traphagen who first recovered his senses. What a cool, wary, calculating, cold-blooded demon that man really was at heart! I blushed for my sex as he began to speak.

"' Before the match is awarded to Mr. Rivers,' said this scurvy fellow, ' I should like to call your attention, Mr. Referee, to the following memoranda of the play for this last hole. According to my notes, whose correctness will be vouched for by McPherson, my caddie, Mr. Rivers teed a *Henley* ball for his drive. He made his second shot with a *Silvertown*, and used an *O. K.* for his third. The fourth, fifth, sixth, and seventh were made respectively with a *Thornton*, a *Woodley Flier*, a *Melfort*, and a *Tom Morris*, and I dare say that the one now in the cup is of still another make, possibly a *Musselburgh*. I submit that Mr. Rivers has lost at least half a dozen balls in playing the hole, and I therefore claim hole and match, according to the rules of golf."

"Gracious heavens! Rivers had plainly neglected the obvious precaution of providing himself with only one make of balls, and his folly made the proof of the harmless deception only too easy. This, then, explained the careful examination that Traphagen had made of his adversary's ball before each shot. No doubt he was right, but how contemptible this underhand, cowardly espionage seemed now in the light of that last brilliant, glorious stroke by which Rivers had redeemed himself! My decision was quickly made; I would not allow low cunning to triumph over genius. I briefly pointed out that objections of this nature must be made immediately upon the discovery of the offence. Had Mr. Traphagen called my attention at the time to any one of these surreptitiously introduced balls, I should, of course, have awarded him the match. But there could be no *ex post facto* evidence introduced. By his previous silence the plaintiff had lost his right to protest.

"'But that last ball that Mr. Rivers played was a spare one of my own,' said Traphagen, with suppressed fury; 'a *Musselburgh*, stamped with my initials. I dropped it myself in the hazard.'

"'Then you gave the misinformation yourself,' I retorted, calmly, 'and by Rule 27 Mr. Rivers cannot be held responsible. The ball now in the hole wins the match for the player who put it there, and it is the only evidence that I can accept.'

"And then, if you will believe it, a doubt, sudden, horrible, sickening, came over me. I ran to the cup and looked in. *The hole was empty; the ball had disappeared.*

"That settled it, of course. It made no difference that we had all distinctly seen the ball as it ran into the hole. It certainly was not there now, and the absolute proof was wanting that it had ever really been there. It was a fitting

dénouement to the extraordinary inci-
dents of an extraordinary match. I
could not go back upon my own words,
and with a heavy heart I formally
awarded the match to Traphagen. Just
then I noticed that Mrs. Chase had disappeared. She had vanished as completely as the lost ball. Was it a coincidence?

"I saw Traphagen take Rivers to one
side and slip a roll of bills into his hand.
His triumphant expression was inde-
scribably odious to me, and my heart
went out to Rivers. The latter turned
away to his trap without a word, and
I followed and jumped in with him. I
would stick by him to the last.

"On the way to the station Rivers
told me briefly of the real nature of the
wager that had been at stake. I could
but press his hand in silent sympathy.
Of Mrs. Chase I would not trust myself
to speak.

"We drove up to the station, and the
hackman shouldered Rivers's portman-

"AND THERE STOOD MRS. EDNA SEVERN CHASE"

teau — each man, you see, had been
obliged to prepare himself for the
worst. In silence we entered the
dreary, ill-lighted waiting-room, and
there stood Mrs. Edna Severn Chase,
looking particularly fit in her neat trav-
elling-suit, and behind her the effulgent
face of old Judge Brown, justice of the
peace for Marion County.

"'We have just five minutes before
the train is due,' remarked Mrs. Chase,
coolly, 'and so, Mr. Rivers, if you are
still of the same mind, and would like
to have me accompany you, Mr. Brown
is ready to oblige. And, by-the-way,'
turning to me and holding out a small
round object, 'you might give this to
Mr. Traphagen, with my compliments.'
I took it, and it was a *Musselburgh* golf-
ball stamped with the initials J. T.

"'Then it was you—you—' stammered Rivers.

"'Certainly. I took it out of the hole
and carried it away while you all were
disputing over those stupid rules.'

"'But I don't see yet—' began Rivers.

"'Why, you foolish boy, if you hadn't lost the match we shouldn't have had Mr. Traphagen's two hundred and fifty dollars upon which to enjoy a wedding-trip. You haven't the most distant notions about economy. Do be reasonable, and if you really want me—'

"Well, I could have married her myself at that instant, she looked so adorable, and Rivers at last managed to rise to the situation. Justice Brown tied the knot with his accustomed skill, and then the north-bound express thundered in, and I helped the bride up the steps of the sleeping-car, and stood alone watching the red end-lights as they disappeared in the darkness."

The *Ancient* stopped, and pulled reflectively at his pipe. The *Man-in-the-Corner* spoke up :

"What did Mr. James Traphagen say when you gave him the ball ?"

"What did he say ? What did he say ?" snorted the *Ancient*. "I don't

"'THIS IS ALL ON ME'"

think that you ought to ask such a question, young man. His language was not intended for publication. But I'll tell you what he did. He took his Philp putter, the only genuine one that ever came to this country, went out on the railway embankment, and bashed rock ballast with it all afternoon. But perhaps it was just as well, for otherwise he might have exploded in here and damaged the club-house."

"This is all on me," said the *Man-in-the-Corner*, softly, as Peter came in with the order-card.

THE PRIME GREAT SECRET

THE PRIME GREAT SECRET

"No such thing as the prime great secret, eh?"

It was the *Silent Member* who spoke, a rare occurrence in itself and one to command attention, but there was something more than mere words in the sentence that has just been recorded. The *Fiend* hastened to take up the challenge.

"No, sir; the prime great secret is but the baseless fable of a duffer's dream, our twentieth-century substitute for the philosopher's stone, and equally elusive and unsubstantial. Golf, with all things else in nature, has its fixed laws, its immutable limitations—"

THE PRIME GREAT SECRET

"Most assuredly," retorted the *Silent Member;* "I have watched your game long enough to know that. Limitations, indeed! As it happens, your particular golfing cult is founded upon Sir Walter Simpson's 'categorical imperative,' and 'hitting the ball' is the sum and substance of all your efforts. Given that as a premise and we arrive, through process of logic, at the following beautiful paradox : the oftener the ball is hit, the fewer strokes it will take to do the round. For a concrete illustration we will examine your score - card for last Saturday's medal play."

The *Silent Member* walked over to the bulletin-board. "Here it is," he went on. "You hit the ball on that occasion no fewer than one hundred and thirty-seven times. Now what does that prove?"

"Nothing," growled the *Fiend.* "You know perfectly well that I broke my play-club at the third hole."

"But you continued to hit the ball," persisted the *Silent Member.*

"Of course I did," roared the *Fiend*, goaded to madness under this indecent application of the *argumentum ad hominem*, "but somehow the confounded thing wouldn't go."

"Precisely. Then you must acknowledge that there is something in *how* you hit the ball if it is to go."

"Well, and what then?"

"Oh, that *how* is the prime great secret."

"Indeed," sneered the *Fiend*. "Possibly you speak from the vantage-ground of a personal experience."

The *Silent Member* smiled, but there was an infinite sadness in the lines about his mouth. "I do," he said, simply. Then he opened the door and went out.

For some moments nobody spoke. The tremendous significance of the *Silent Member's* categorical affirmation was more than overwhelming; it was paralyzing. And that last look in his eyes as he turned and closed the door!

There was a despair in it, a freezing hopelessness, that was almost physical in its effects upon those who encountered it. Robinson Brown actually shivered and his chair creaked noisily as he leaned forward and held his hands close above the crackling logs.

Woodehouse was the first to recover himself. "What rot!" he remarked, sententiously.

"Why, the old man, to my certain knowledge, has never had a club in his hand," put in Egerton, "and I've been a member here for fifteen years. How about it, *Ancient ?*"

"He was one of the charter members," returned the Oracle, placidly, "and dates back to '93 or thereabouts."

"A quarter of a century, then," said the *Fiend*, making a rapid mental calculation. "That's a long time to live without playing golf. I always thought that there was something uncanny about the man."

"It's equivalent to a stroke or hole to

have him in the gallery," said Robinson Brown, decidedly. "I can't play a little bit if I see him looking on. He always seems to know what a fellow ought not to do, just before he goes and does it."

The impressiveness of this concluding statement was somewhat marred by its lack of lucidity, and only Mr. Brown's fellow-members in Class C appeared able to grapple with its subtle significance. They beamed complacently upon each other and interchanged unutterable winks. Evidently there is a secret understanding among duffers.

"It isn't hypnotism, either," remarked Alderson, thoughtfully. "He doesn't try to interfere in any way with a man's play, but there is something in that serene, immovable, omniscient gaze of his that is absolutely fatal to my holing-out. It makes me feel as though I were about to read a paper at the Twilight Club upon the mistakes in the Pentateuch, and had suddenly looked up and recognized Moses sitting by the door."

"Well, in my opinion," interrupted the *Fiend*, warmly, "it's most confoundedly impertinent of him. For a man who, as the *Ancient* said, has been a member here for twenty - five years and has never had a club in his hand—"

"But I never said any such thing," interrupted the *Ancient*, in his turn. "If you'll look back over the records you'll see his name often enough. Madison Grimshaw, captain of the club from 1893 to 1899; third man at the open meeting in 1896; runner-up at Chicago in 1897; six open - tournament cups in 1898, and the silver medal at the amateur championship, same year; drawn against Elphinstone of Peconic in the amateur finals of 1899, and withdrew— there the record stops."

"Well, of all things!" and the *Fiend* drew in his breath sharply. "M. Grimshaw, our *Silent Member*, *he* the Madison Grimshaw of those six glorious years, the golden age of the Marion County Club! You can't mean it?"

"But I do; he is Madison Grimshaw."

"But—but I thought—that is, I always understood—there was a catastrophe, something tragic—went under in a big match, didn't he? Apoplexy, or perhaps it was collapse. All the papers were full of it. I can just remember the excitement in the air."

"If you want the truth about it," said the *Ancient*, slowly, "it was simply a case of too much prime great secret."

"Then there is such a thing?"

"Unquestionably."

"And Grimshaw possessed it?"

"Without a doubt; and he has it still?"

"But—but he never uses it."

"He never did use it but once, and that is just where the story comes in."

"Fire away," said the *Fiend*, with an air of tolerant scepticism. "Of course you won't expect us to believe the fairy-tale?"

"Certainly not," retorted the *Ancient*. "I don't expect anything of a man who tees his ball in a bunker, and yet has never done the course under triple figures. Let me say, however, that I simply propose to state the facts, and not to comment upon them. Have I the floor?"

The privilege was immediately accorded, and the *Fiend*, under threat of being gagged with an old ball if he ventured upon any interruption, retired to a distant corner and affected to busy himself with the *Golfing Annual*. But Woodehouse kept an eye upon him; there is jealousy even among the wretched duffers of Class C, and he suspected that the *Fiend* was hardly so indifferent as his actions would imply. One may smile at the idea of a prime great secret in golf, and yet be a villain.

"As I have said," began the old gentleman, "our Grimshaw was indeed *the* Grimshaw of glorious memory, and the crack amateur of his day. It was remarkable how quickly he picked up the game, and since to natural genius

he added an infinite capacity for taking pains, it is no wonder that he was
soon at the top of the tree. In Grimshaw the Marion County Club had developed a really first - class man, and
when the amateur championship meeting for 1899 was awarded to us, we all
felt confident that our champion had
more than an even chance to win out.

"Well, at the end of the second day's
play it was pretty plain that the contest
for the gold medal lay between Grimshaw and McLeod, an ex-Hoylake player
and short - odds man. It was the old
story of native skill against imported
talent, and for the first time the chances
seemed to be slightly in our favor. The
luck of the draw kept the men apart
until the semi-finals, when they were
paired against each other; the second
couple being Elphinstone of Peconic
and Hawley of Rollwood. Both Elphinstone and Hawley were decidedly
second-string men, who had managed
to pull off their earlier matches through

technical rulings, aided by unexpected reversals in form on the part of their opponents. It was a foregone conclusion that the survivor of the Grimshaw-McLeod match would be the amateur champion of 1899, and the interest consequently centred upon that contest. And upon the form already shown Grimshaw had been backed to win.

"Now I had been carrying for Grimshaw. He had great confidence in my judgment, although I was by no means a crack in actual performance, and he had the idea that I could steady him at a crisis better than anybody else, professional or what not. Of course I was doing my best to pull him through, both out of club loyalty and from personal friendship.

"The match in the third round was a win for Grimshaw by five up and four to play, which looked very fair on paper, McLeod being a strong player, but somehow I fancied that the strain of the tournament was beginning to tell upon my man. There were little signs of weakness and indecision in his play, indicating that something was wrong. Of course it might be merely a temporary falling off, but I began to feel a bit anxious. Naturally I kept my misgivings to myself; it would have been madness to even hint at them to Grimshaw.

"I had been spending the tournament week at Grimshaw's house, and on that particular Thursday night he had gone up-stairs at an early hour, presumably bound for bed. A long night's rest was exactly what he needed, and I was consequently annoyed when I came up, a couple of hours later, to notice that a light was still burning in his bedroom. I knocked and then entered, without waiting for an answer. The room and bed were empty. I glanced over at the corner where he kept his clubs, and— merciful heavens!—the bag was gone. What insanity of folly was this? Midnight practice before a crucial match! We were lost indeed; I knew the match was McLeod's as surely as though I had seen it posted upon the bulletin-board. I sank into a chair, crushed, broken-hearted. It was now half-past twelve.

"The clock struck one, the door opened, and Grimshaw stood before me. I could hardly believe my senses. There was a new light in his eyes and an assured smile upon his lips that made him look like the Grimshaw of old; something had happened to restore his moral tone, some miracle had given him back his pristine confidence in himself. I waited for the explanation.

"Grimshaw placed his bag of clubs in the corner, sat down opposite to me, and prepared to light a cigarette. Cigarettes !—the rankest of poisons to a man of his temperament. I looked my blackest disapproval.

"'Go easy, old man,' he began, coolly. 'It's all right; everything is all right, for I have the prime great secret, direct from *Col. Bogey* himself. I got it at the thirteenth hole not half an hour ago.'"

"Worse and worse! if this were really the explanation of his altered demeanor. Poor fellow! it was only too evident that his mind was giving way under the awful strain of the tournament. Ah, this Juggernaut of golf!

"'You don't believe me,' said Grimshaw, looking at me steadily. 'Well, what do you make of that?' and he put into my hand a small round object."

The *Ancient* stopped, and, fumbling in his waistcoat pocket, produced a wooden box, which he solemnly handed to Alderson for inspection. It went from hand to hand around the circle, and Woodehouse examined it with especial interest. In shape it resembled a pill-box, and it was made of some foreign-looking, close-grained wood, very dark in color and highly polished. Upon the lid was a couplet in black-letter, and Woodehouse slowly spelled it out:

"'Once for far and once for sure,
And once for what is past alle cure.'"

The *Ancient* reached for the box, dropped it carelessly into an outside pocket, and resumed his story.

"'Open it,' said Grimshaw.

"I did so, and saw that it contained a curious-looking paste, or rather salve. It had an aromatic odor, not unpleasant, but quite unknown to me. Part of the contents had been used, and now I could detect that same peculiar odor hanging about Grimshaw himself.

"'Well?' and I looked at him expectantly.

"'I may as well tell the whole truth,' he blurted out. 'But first look at this,' and he handed me a parchment-bound volume evidently of great age. It was in black-letter, and purported to be a treatise on Black Magic, printed at Leyden in 1527 by Carolus Nuyse, for Magister Claudius Paraloubomatos, of the Academy of Universal Science.

"'What nonsense is this?' I said, frowningly.

"'Read,' said Grimshaw, pointing to a marked paragraph.

"' Lette duffers toppe and duffers sclaffe,
  The prime greate secret of the gowffe,
  The Bogey-Manne shalle give the wight
  Who dares to playe, on moonless night,

"'The Thirteen Hole from greene to tee;
  A deede of darkeness foul, pardie.
  So once for far and once for sure,
  And once for what is past alle cure.'

"I lost my patience completely at this gibberish, and, shutting the book with a bang, I told Grimshaw plainly that if he did not instantly throw away that cigarette and go to bed he would have to find some one else to carry for him on the morrow. He listened to me exactly as though I were some fractious child who had to be coaxed into good-humor, and then said, quietly:

"' Just as you please, old man. I absolve you from all responsibility; but you have got to hear the story, and you may as well resign yourself. Come in.'

"There was a knock at the door, and his man Pollock entered, bearing a supper-tray. I groaned aloud. Welsh rarebits and grilled bones! Well, nothing could matter now, and as I am very fond of a bone I resumed my seat and held out my plate.

"'When I came up-stairs this evening,' began Grimshaw, 'I had every intention of going to bed at once, and in fact I did get half undressed. But I soon discovered that I was too unstrung to hope for sleep; that infernal match with McLeod kept getting on my nerves, and I knew as certainly as I am sitting here that I would go to pieces to-morrow; I was a beaten man before the match. In desperation I pulled a chair before the fire, took down at random a book from the case, and determined to distract my mind, if such a thing were possible, by an hour of hard reading. The book was this curious old volume that I had picked up at a Seine bookstall last summer, and of course the first thing I saw was the doggerel verse that you have just read. The prime great secret ! Could there really be such a thing ? and then that odd fancy of playing the thirteenth hole backwards on a moonless night ! Somehow the ridiculous old formula so gravely set down by the learned Magister Claudius Paraloubomatos began to take hold of my imagination. And then desperate cases— you know the old saying. I was more excited now than ever, and with that jingle ringing in my ears I would not stop to reason with myself. The almanac told me that the moon would be down ; my bicycle was in the stable ; you fellows were making such a row in the billiard-room that it was an easy matter to get out of the house without being overheard, and before I knew it I was on my way to the golf club.

"'The course was entirely deserted, but the night was not absolutely dark, and I had no difficulty in making my way to the fateful thirteenth hole. I

threw down a ball upon McPherson's precious turf and took my brassey. Then
for the moment my courage failed me.
To drive a ball off a putting-green! It
was an act akin to sacrilege, and my
knees knocked together with horror at
the unholy deed. And then some fiend
whispered McLeod's name in my ear,
and my nerves grew steady again. You
know how I loathe the beast; let me be
eternally bunkered now but I would
play out this devil's game to the last
stroke.

"'I brought the brassey down with a
vicious jab that left a horrible howk
upon the velvet surface of the green.
But I only laughed aloud, and followed
after the ball with a light-hearted reck-
lessness that henceforth would stop at
nothing. I even hummed a tune as I
prepared to take my second.

"'As you know, the thirteenth is a
short hole and the *Sheol* bunker is some
fifty yards in front of the tee. As I was
playing the hole backwards, I was, of

course, approaching the bunker from behind—going into *Sheol* by the back-door, as it were. I did my best to clear the hazard, but topped, and the ball rolled up close against the bunker, a duffer shot that annoyed me exceeding-ly. I went to where the ball had struck, but it was not to be seen. But right there, on the edge of the bunker's cliff, was that small box, together with what appeared to be a gentleman's vis-iting-card. I picked up the latter, and immediately dropped it with a yell, for it was white-hot. The turf actually sizzled where it fell, and a light smoke arose as the card slowly curled up and resolved itself into ashes. But in the mean time I had been able to make out the writing upon it: "*The Prime Great Secret, with the compliments of Colonel Bogey. Use only as directed.*"

"'The box was warm, but not un-pleasantly so, and on opening it I found it full of the strange ointment that you have already seen. Evidently it was to be rubbed in somewhere, and, after a moment's hesitation, I bared my left arm and applied a small portion. It had an immediate and astonishing effect. The muscles and tendons of my arm felt as though they had been suddenly endowed with new vigor and elasticity. I had the strength of a Samson in that left arm, and on putting it to a practical test I was amazed to see how far I could now drive a ball. Two, three hundred yards were as nothing; endowed with this supernatural strength I would not be afraid to measure clubs with Jehu himself.

"'This was all very well, but I soon noticed that my shots were hardly so straight as they were far, and that my short game left much to be desired. Struck by a new thought, I read again the couplet upon the box lid. "Once for far and once for sure"—yes, that was it; I must make a second application of the salve if I desired the equally important secret of unfailing accuracy.

This time I anointed my right arm, the one that guides the club, and I was delighted to find that now I was as sure as I had been far. Straight as an arrow flew every drive; my quarter-shots had just the right pitch and cut; and my putting was invariably up and straight. Far and sure: what more could be desired? *I had the prime great secret.* I tried a few more shots simply to assure myself of the reality of my good fortune, and then, gathering up my clubs, I started for home, and here I am.'

"I was about to speak, but Grimshaw stopped me.

"'There is nothing to be gained by discussing this remarkable occurrence,' he said, airily. 'But you can rest assured that I am going to beat McLeod out in the semi-finals, and in the mean time I'm off to bed. Hello! half-past one! Well, good-night, and tell the boys that they can back me to the limit.'

"Grimshaw rose, yawned, threw away

his cigarette, walked over to the alcove, and disappeared behind the curtains. I could hear him throw off his clothes and jump into bed. In ten minutes more he was breathing regularly, and, looking in, I could see that he was sleeping as peacefully as any child.

"Well, what was I to make of this cock-and-bull story? It was no use puzzling my brains over it; the fact remained that Grimshaw, in some inexplicable manner, had recovered his lost nerve and old-time confidence in himself. He now believed that he could beat McLeod, and that was the all-important point. And so, with some of his new-born confidence insensibly communicated to my own mind, I in turn retired to rest.

"As to the semi-finals, I need only say that Grimshaw's play was superb, and that he beat McLeod at that same thirteenth hole by six up and five to play. As we came up to the green I noticed with a shiver a long jagged skelp upon its smooth surface. It was a cruel, gaping wound, and to my excited imagination it had the appearance of evil lips parted into a mocking and hateful smile. There was something appallingly sinister in that diabolical grin, something unearthly, if I may be allowed the expression, and I felt decidedly uncomfortable and even a bit shaky about the knees. But Grimshaw only winked at me, and suggested to the chairman of the Green Committee that McPherson, the green-keeper, was in urgent need of a sound wigging.

"Elphinstone beat his man, and this left him in the finals with Grimshaw on Saturday. There could be no earthly doubt of the result, so we celebrated the discounted victory in the club-house that same night. Grimshaw was the hero of the occasion, and we were all wildly enthusiastic over the anticipated triumph. There were actually some wagers laid that Grimshaw would win without losing a single hole, and El-

phinstone was so admittedly outclassed
that his friends were privately urging
his withdrawal. But he was an obstinate fellow, and insisted upon playing it
out. Plucky but foolish, we thought
him.

"The contestants were to drive off
for the thirty - six - hole match at ten
o'clock, and although there could be but
little interest in the match itself, the
'gallery' was fully as large as ever, it
having been noised about that Grimshaw was to try and make a new record
for the course. The hour came, and I
went into the dressing-room to call him.
I found him standing at the window
with his sleeves rolled up and the mysterious box in his hand. He greeted
me with a smile, and said, cheerfully,
'Just another touch of this divine stuff
and I think I can get down to seventy-
two for the first round.'

"'Hold on,' I said, taking the box
from him. 'Better leave well enough
alone.'

" 'Nonsense! What possible harm can it do? I have the prime great secret, my boy, and I intend to smash that record into infinitesimal bits. The prime great secret! Ha! ha!' and he hummed gayly,

" 'Once for far and once for sure,
  And once for what is past alle cure.'

"He put out his hand for the fatal box.

" 'Grimshaw, you fool,' I almost shouted, 'don't you see the warning in those very words? If the doggerel means anything at all, you will repent it if you apply the ointment the third time. Don't you remember the story in the *Arabian Nights* of the covetous Baba Abdalla and the magic salve that the dervish gave him? The application to his right eye revealed to him all the riches of the earth, but, not content, he insisted upon trying it upon the left eye, and was stricken blind. "Once for far and once for sure!" What can be farther than far? what can be surer than sure? "And once for what is past alle cure." I tell you to beware.'

"'Pooh!' retorted Grimshaw; 'the meaning is obvious enough. It is the record that is to be past all cure after I have finished smashing it. Give me that box, I say,' and then, before I could interpose another word, he had snatched it from me and had smeared the salve liberally upon both his arms.

"Perhaps I had expected that he would fall in a fit or collapse in some other dreadful fashion, but apparently the application had no effect whatever. He stood there with a play club in his hand and tried a couple of swings.

"'Well?' and I looked at him anxiously.

"'It stings, rather,' he answered, shortly; 'but that's nothing. Let's get out.'

"As you know, there is a bunker some forty yards in front of the first tee; we used to call it the *Asses' Bridge*

in the old days. Elphinstone drove off
and cleared it nicely, and then Grimshaw stepped to the tee. He looked fit
to play for his life, and it was all that
the Green Committee could do to sup-
press the continuous hand-clapping that
ran up and down the line like a dis-
charge of musketry. Finally, quiet was
restored, Grimshaw swung back, then
down upon the ball, and, oh, merciful
heavens !—

"I won't give you the details," resumed the *Ancient*, recovering his com-
posure by a supreme effort, "but at the
forty-seventh fruitless stroke some of
his friends went down into the bunker
and led him quietly but firmly back to
the club-house. And the name of that
bunker is *Grimshaw's Grave* unto this
day."

The *Ancient* stopped, and his faded
blue eyes were full of unshed tears as he
turned his head away. The memory of
that awful moment was still fresh in the
old man's faithful heart, and we could

not but respect his display of feeling and old-time loyalty to his unhappy friend.

It was Alderson who finally mustered courage to put the question we were all dying to ask.

" But the prime great secret—it was gone, of course ?"

" Not at all. He still possessed it in all its fulness and virtue, and he has it to this day. He knows the game and how to play it as no mortal man has ever done or ever will."

" But he never plays."

" And he never has played since that unlucky morning."

" I don't quite follow you."

"' Once for far and once for sure,
And once for what is past alle cure,'"

quoted the *Ancient*, solemnly. " The directions were precise and absolutely truthful. The first application of the salve endued Madison Grimshaw with superhuman driving power, the second gave him supernatural accuracy, and the third—*the golf elbow*."

The *Ancient* rose and left the smoking-room, and one by one the company followed him in silence until Woodehouse and the *Fiend* were left alone. The keen eye of Woodehouse had noticed that the little box had fallen from the old gentleman's pocket as he rose, and that it was now lying under the table. The *Fiend* appeared to be absorbed in his reading, and Woodehouse made a stealthy move towards the coveted object. The *Fiend* looked up suddenly, and Woodehouse yawned elaborately and walked to a window.

There! the *Fiend's* eyes were riveted again upon his book. Woodehouse took a tentative step in the direction of the table, and the *Fiend* was reading harder than ever. Woodehouse felt encouraged, lounged carelessly up to the table, and filled his match-safe. Still no movement on the part of the enemy. Woodehouse purposely dropped his match-safe and stooped as though to recover it. The precious box was in his grasp; he straightened up ; but there was an iron grip upon his wrist, and a sullen, baleful glance met his own.

" Halves !" hissed the *Fiend* between his clinched teeth as they faced each other.

Woodehouse hesitated a moment, but he knew the *Fiend* full well. He nodded and removed the lid. A faint spicy odor could be sensibly detected, but that was all. *The box was empty.*

" G-r-r-r !" snarled the *Fiend*. " I knew there was nothing in it."

  *   *   *   *   *

Extract from the minutes of the Executive Committee, June 26, 19—:

" McPherson, the green-keeper, reported that on Tuesday night last he had occasion to cross the course at a late hour, when he was surprised to see a man standing at the thirteenth hole with a club in his hand. On approaching he recognized in him Mr. G. Graham, a member of the club, and otherwise known as the *Fiend.* To the green-keeper's amazement and horror he distinctly saw Mr. Graham proceed to drive a ball off the putting-green with his brassey, incidentally howking up the turf in a most outrageous manner. After a sharp personal encounter he succeeded in obtaining possession of Mr. Graham's club, and to prevent any further injury to the course he took it upon himself to lock up the gentleman overnight in the tool-house. It was resolved that McPherson should be presented with a twenty-dollar gold piece in recognition of his prompt and commendable action, and, upon motion of Mr. Woodehouse, Mr. Graham was unanimously expelled from the membership of the club."

*   *   *   *   *

Woodehouse came into the club the other day and announced that he was through with golf. "It's both effeminate and faddish," he asserted, in his toploftiest manner, "and in future I shall go in for something intellectual, like chess, the king of games, don't you know."

"Good idea," assented Alderson, with

a wink at Robinson Brown. "Chess is undoubtedly the game for a man who carries his left arm in a sling."

"Do you mean to insinuate—" began Woodehouse, getting very red in the face.

"Not for the world, my dear fellow. Still, it is not an unheard-of thing for *two* moths to get singed at the same candle."

THE END